Empty Eyes

A SCREENPLAY

by

Niko Zinovii

Zinovii Art Studio

Santa Monica, California

chrysos

Published by: Zinovii Art Studio
Santa Monica, California
www.zinoviiartstudio.com

ISBN: 978-0-9900085-4-5   (trade paperback)

LCCN: 2020906319

Cover art by: Leonardo Ariel Ariza Ardila
Cover art Copyright © 2020 by Niko Zinovii

First Edition, 2020
Printed in the United States of America

Dedication

To the young at heart

This screenplay is also dedicated with love to the memory of
Jeannette S.

Contents

A Note on the Screenplay

The screenplay that follows is reproduced in its entirety and unaltered, with only slight adjustments made to its original format in order to provide greater ease of reading; specifically, script page numbers and scene numbers have been eliminated, as have all the uses of "(CONTINUED)" and "CONTINUED:" and "MORE" that delineate the continuation of scenes and dialogue across ordinal pages.

As this book is of a smaller size than a standard 8 ½" x 11" screenplay, each page of script no longer represents one minute of screen time. (The *Empty Eyes* screenplay in its original 8 ½" x 11" size is 115 pages in length.)

EXT indicates an outdoor scene, INT and indoor scene. O.S. is an abbreviation for "off screen."

Niko Zinovii

Act One

Niko Zinovii

FADE IN:

EXT. FARMHOUSE AND FIELDS - DAWN

The sun is rising, its soft, early morning rays bathing an attractive farmhouse that is surrounded by planted fields and a half dozen barns and sheds. A long, lonely road runs by the front of the farmstead.

"KANSAS... THE NEAR FUTURE" appears upon the screen, the words disappearing moments later.

EXT. FARMHOUSE ROOF - DAWN

A gentle breeze turns an old silver weather vane. Shaped like a man, its metal face turns toward the rising sun. Two cut out circles, representing eyes, are the vane's only facial features.

Somewhere O.S. a rooster crows.

The **FILM'S TITLE "EMPTY EYES"** appears upon the screen, disappearing soon after.

EXT. BARNYARD - DAWN

A **ROOSTER**, atop a bail of hay, crows out again.

INT. CHILDREN'S BEDROOM - DAWN

<u>**CREDITS BEGIN**</u>

The rooster's cry ends. **JENNIFER**, a happy ten-year-old girl, awakens. She jumps upon her younger brother's bed.

> **JENNIFER**
> Nicholas, wake up, it's mornin'.

NICHOLAS, a five year old with adorable deep blue eyes, awakens.

> **JENNIFER**
> Come-on, get out of bed you sleepy head. Don't you want to go play with the puppies?

> **NICHOLAS**
> Yeah, the puppies.

INT. PARENT'S BEDROOM - DAWN

ANDREW and **LISA**, the children's parents, are sleeping close to each other. Both are in their 40s, attractive, caring, and intelligent.

The bedroom door creaks and slowly opens. Standing in the hall are the children. Jennifer is dressed; Nicholas is still in his pajamas.

> **JENNIFER**
> Mom.

She stirs but does not awaken.

> **JENNIFER**
> Mom.

Lisa awakens, sitting up.

> **LISA**
> Jennifer? What's wrong?

> **JENNIFER**
> Wake up and help Nicholas get dressed.

Lisa looks at the time.

LISA
Honey, its not even 5:30.

JENNIFER
We got up early to go
play with the puppies.

LISA
To play with the puppies?
The puppies are sleeping
honey, you can't go
waking them up. They're
like babies, they need
their rest, to grow.

JENNIFER
Well, then we just want
to look at them. Come-on
Mom, help Nicholas get
dressed.

LISA
Jennifer, your Mom is
very tired. Why don't you
dress Nicholas?

JENNIFER
Mom... That's your job.

Lisa smiles.

> **LISA**
> My job.
> (A beat)
> I tell you what, why
> don't you go wakeup Clark
> and have him help
> Nicholas. I think he has
> to get up soon
> anyway.Okay?

Jennifer does not answer right away.

> **JENNIFER**
> Okay.

Jennifer closes the bedroom door. Lisa
lies back down, smiling.

> **LISA**
> "That's your job."

CREDITS END

EXT. BACK PORCH - DAY

CLARK is tying Nicholas's shoes.
Jennifer is watching. Clark is a good-
looking 15-year-old who is smart,
responsible, and wholesome.

CLARK

Okay, there, you're all
set.

NICHOLAS

Thanks Clark.

CLARK

Hey, what's a big brother
for.

JENNIFER

Come-on Nicholas.

CLARK

Wait, hold on. Now
Jennifer, I've got to go
so I want you to take
Number 4 with you, okay?

The children do not like this at all.

JENNIFER

What?

CLARK

Look, Mom and Dad are
still sleeping and I
don't want you two
getting into any trouble
this morning. Remember
last week when you broke

that window?

JENNIFER
That was an accident.

CLARK
Take Number 4.

JENNIFER
Oh, I don't want to. He's
no fun. All he does is
order us around.

NICHOLAS
Yeah, he won't let us do
anything.

CLARK
Take Number 4 or stay
inside until Mom gets up.

JENNIFER
But —

CLARK
— No buts.
     (A beat)
So, what is it? Inside or
Number 4?

JENNIFER
... Number 4...

                    CLARK
          You promise?

Jennifer crosses her fingers behind her
back.

                   JENNIFER
          I promise.

Clark notices her hands behind her back.

                    CLARK
          Crosses don't count.

                   JENNIFER
          Okay, okay. Crosses don't
          count. Come-on Nicholas,
          let's go get Number 4.

Jennifer stomps off.

                  NICHOLAS
          See you later Clark.

Clark runs a hand over Nicholas's head.

                    CLARK
          See you later punk.

Nicholas laughs and skips after
Jennifer.

Clark walks a futuristic ten-speed bicycle - that sports a cool plastic windshield - toward the road.

EXT. FARMHOUSE AND FIELDS - DAY

Clark is pedaling down the road. The children are moving toward a barnyard behind the house.

EXT. ROAD - DAY

Clark pedals away.

EXT. BARNYARD - DAY

Nicholas is following Jennifer toward a small barn.

> **NICHOLAS**
> Jennifer, wait up.

Jennifer does not comply, stomping into the barn.

> **NICHOLAS**
> Jennifer.

INT. SMALL BARN - DAY

Jennifer walks over to **SIX SHADOWED FIGURES**, seated besides each other on a long bench. Slumped forward, they are solemn and lifeless.

Jennifer turns on the lights revealing the figures to be robots. Human-like in shape, they are nearly identical. Their silver-gray metal bodies are lean, their waists wasp-like, being no more than six to eight inches in diameter. Their joints are hinged. They have a narrow slit where a mouth should be and small holes for ears. Their eyes are large, circular, and made of thick, lifeless glass. The tops of their heads are encased by plastic, egg shaped, transparent domes, displaying their computerized brains. Their hands are skeleton-like.

On the chest of each robot is a number, corresponding to the order in which they are seated, numbered 1 through 6. Jennifer steps over to Number 4, looking at the robot with disdain. Nicholas steps up besides her.

JENNIFER
Stupid robot.

NICHOLAS
Jennifer, don't turn him on. He won't let us have any fun.

JENNIFER
I have to, I promised.
And Dad always says that
you have to keep your
word.

Jennifer pulls a large plug out of the
robot's left leg. Reluctantly, she then
pushes in the button that is in the
center of the robot's chest. Immediately
the robot's brain lights up beneath its
transparent encasement. It sits upright
and looks at the children. The robot's
voice is masculine but pleasant and
completely without emotion.

NUMBER 4
Good morning Jennifer and
Nicholas. Today is Thursday, July
the eleventh, the one hundred
and ninety second day of this
year. There are one hundred and
seventy three days remaining.

The children exchange disapproving
glances.

NUMBER 4
It is five fifty six am. Why are you
both awake and outdoors at this
time?

JENNIFER

We woke up early to see the puppies, and Clark said that we had to bring you with us.

NUMBER 4

Does Mrs. Reeves know that you are planning to visit the young of her canine mammal?

JENNIFER

Our dog has a name you know. You don't have to call her a "canine mammal."

NUMBER 4

The description is accurate.

JENNIFER

I don't think so.

NUMBER 4

Jennifer, I am awaiting your answer.

JENNIFER

Yes, she knows.

NUMBER 4

Good, I will accompany you.

The robot rises to its feet.

NUMBER 4
Let us proceed.

The robot starts walking off. The hinges
on its knees, hips, ankles, and feet
squeak with each step it takes. Its
movements are ridged and very
mechanical.

NUMBER 4
Come along children.

Reluctantly, the children follow the
robot.

JENNIFER
Next time we sneak out
without waking up Clark.

NICHOLAS
Who will tie my shoes?

JENNIFER
I will.

EXT. BARNYARD - DAY

The robot exits the barn and slows its
pace, allowing the children to catch up.
Nicholas eyes the hinges on the robot's
knees.

                    NICHOLAS
          I don't like the sound he
          makes when he walks. It
          bothers my ears.

The robot continues looking straight
ahead, displaying no reaction to the
boy's comment.

                    JENNIFER
          I don't like his eyes.
          The way he looks at us
          with those glass eyes.
                    (A beat)
          He's not real. He's not
          really alive.

Continuing to look straight ahead the
robot displays no reaction.

EXT. PEN ON OTHER SIDE OF BARNYARD - DAY

A **GERMAN SHEPHERD DOG** and her **PUPPIES**
are in a fenced pen, lying on a bed of
straw. The puppies are wrestling one
another, maneuvering for position on
their mother's teats.

The robot and the children are
approaching. Jennifer and Nicholas run
ahead, rushing up to the pen. They stick
their arms into the pen, playing with

the puppies. The mother German Shepherd greets the children.

> **JENNIFER**
> Hi Cleopatra. How are
> your puppies today?

Cleopatra licks Jennifer's face with a long wet tongue.

> **JENNIFER**
> Let's climb inside with
> them.
> **NICHOLAS**
> Yeah.

Jennifer wiggles forward, squeezing between the pen's posts as the robot steps up behind them.

> **NICHOLAS**
> Uh-oh.

Nicholas lunges forward, attempting to crawl into the pen. The robot grabs the boy by the seat of his pants with a skeleton-like hand, stopping him.

> **NUMBER 4**
> Nicholas, Jennifer, you are not
> allowed to go into the pen.

The robot reaches for Jennifer. She
quickly pulls herself into the pen,
tearing one of her pant legs on a nail.
The robot straightens, pulling Nicholas
to his feet. Without emotion:

NUMBER 4
Jennifer, you must come out of
the pen immediately. You are not
allowed in there. I will report this to
Mrs. Reeves and inform her of
how you tore your clothing.

Jennifer rises to her feet, angry.

JENNIFER
Yeah, just like you
squealed on me for
breakin' that window.

NUMBER 4
Jennifer, you must come out of
the pen immediately.

She thinks for a moment.

JENNIFER
No, I won't.

NUMBER 4
Jennifer, you must come out of
the pen immediately.

JENNIFER
You know, you shouldn't
be telling us what to do,
you're not even real.

NUMBER 4
Jennifer, you must come out of
the pen immediately.

NICHOLAS
Can't he think of
something else to say? He
talks like his head is
empty.

Jennifer stares directly at the robot.

JENNIFER
No... Not his head.
     (A beat)
His eyes. His eyes are
empty.

NUMBER 4
Empty means to contain nothing.
Your use of the word is incorrect
Jennifer.

She gives the robot back its line from
earlier.

JENNIFER
No. The description is
accurate.

She climbs out of the pen and takes
Nicholas by the hand.

NUMBER 4
The description is not accurate
Jennifer, you are mistaken.

Jennifer turns her back to the robot and
pulls Nicholas toward the farmhouse.

JENNIFER
Come-on Nicholas, let's
go back to the house.

She gives the robot a look.

JENNIFER
"Empty Eyes" can follow
us if he wants to.

NUMBER 4
I will accompany you.

The robot follows the children,
unaffected by Jennifer's remarks.

EXT. SOLAR POWER FIELDS - DAY

Huge, rectangular solar mirrors are
covering several hundred acres. Tilted
eastward, the panels are catching the
rays of the rising sun.

A tiny figure on a bike is pedaling down
the lonely highway that runs through the
center of this light-collecting field.

EXT. HIGHWAY - DAY

Coasting, Clark slows the bike,
breaking. Bouncing off the road, he
rolls down toward a small, single story
building.

EXT. SINGLE STORY BUILDING - DAY

As Clark pulls up to the front of the
building and dismounts his bike, **MR.
SMIT**, a hefty man in his mid 40s, steps
out the front door. He is wearing a
white, once piece coverall.

                    CLARK
          Mr. Smit?

                  MR. SMIT
          That's me. Can I help
          you?

Clark reaches forward and shakes Smit's hand.

> **CLARK**
> I'm Clark Reeves. Andrew Reeves' son. You're having a problem with two of your robots?

> **MR. SMIT**
> Three, another went out this morning. — I thought your father was going to be coming out to fix them.

Clark smiles politely.

> **CLARK**
> No, he usually sends me out on calls.

> **MR. SMIT**
> But aren't you a little young to know how to fix these things right? What are you, 16, 17?

Clark tires to maintain his smile.

> **CLARK**
> I'll be 16 next month.

                    MR. SMIT
You're only 15? I don't
believe this. I tell him
that I need these things
fixed right away and he
sends a kid out to do the
job.

                    CLARK
I know what I'm doing
Sir.

Smit eyes him for a moment and then
shrugs his shoulders.

                    MR. SMIT
Well, I sure hope so kid,
these are very expensive
machines. Come-on.

Smit lead Clark around the building.

EXT. BENEATH SOLAR PANELS - DAY

Smit leads Clark away from the building,
walking beneath the solar panels that
are ten feet above their heads,
supported by a vast metal framework.
They walk past several **ROBOTS** that are
performing maintenance duties on one of
the huge panels. These robots are
similar in design to those at the

Reeves' farm but they are leaner and
their heads are flat rather than capped
by transparent domes. They are a
governmental metallic blue in color.

                    CLARK
          P.S.A.s, government
          models. The 300 series?

                    SMIT
          350.

Smit stops in front of two seated,
slumped over, deactivated **ROBOTS**.

                  MR. SMIT
          Go to work.

Clark slips his duffle bag off his
shoulder and pulls out a compact
toolbox. Smit steps back, crosses his
arms, and readies himself to observe the
boy at work. Clark pulls out a small
electric screwdriver and flashes a
nervous smile.

                  MR. SMIT
          Good luck.

                                WIPE TO:

EXT. BENEATH SOLAR PANELS - DAY

One of the robots is walking away from Clark and Smit. Clark is attaching the chest plate back onto the second robot, which remains seated with its head hanging forward. He snaps the chest plate into position and presses the square button in the center of the robot's torso. Immediately the robot starts functioning.

The robot's voice sounds similar to the Reeves robot, Number 4, in that it is masculine and completely without emotion but its delivery is more mechanical, more straight forward, lacking the calm, soothing quality of the Reeves' robot.

> **ROBOT**
> Unit P.S.A. 350-1502 ready for task assignment.

> **CLARK**
> Yeah, it was the AB load switch. These P.S.A.s, they're made kind of cheap. One load switch goes and its entire system shuts down.

Smit smiles.

> **MR. SMIT**
> Well, I've got to hand it
> to you kid — I mean Clark,
> you really do know what
> you're doing. Sorry about
> that before.

> **CLARK**
> That's okay. Where's that
> third one. You said there
> were three.

> **MR. SMIT**
> Oh, I almost forgot, this
> way.
> (To robot)
> Stay there.

Smit walks off, leading Clark deeper
into the field of mirrors.

> **CLARK**
> You know, the Japanese
> R.A.s are built a lot
> better than these and
> they cost about the same.

> **MR. SMIT**
> That's what everybody
> tells me. But, this is a
> government installation
> so it's equipped with

government built robots.
That's just the way
things work — Oh, there
it is.

They walk up to the third robot, which
is seated, deactivated, on the ground.
It looks slightly different from the
robots Clark has just repaired. It is
more streamlined and it looks new.
Printed on the side of its flat head is:
EX. P.S.A. 400

                    CLARK
          P.S.A. 400?

Smit rolls his eyes.

                    MR. SMIT
          "Experimental." It's a
          prototype. They wanted to
          test it out here, see how
          it would do.

                    CLARK
          I take it that it didn't
          do too well.

                    MR. SMIT
          You've got that right.
          The thing acted nutty
          since day one. Like it

didn't have any
programming or something,
I don't know.

CLARK
What happened to it?

MR. SMIT
I turned it off. I think
something's seriously
wrong up there.

He flicks a finger off the robot's metal
head.

MR. SMIT
You probably can't fix it
but I was wondering if
you could take a look.

CLARK
(Eager)
Yeah, sure.

Clark uses his electric screwdriver to
remove the flat metal plate atop the
robot's head. It is attached simply and
it comes off quickly. Clark and Smit
both lean forward, peering into the
robot's small braincase at its complex,
computerized brain.

CLARK

I don't know, everything
looks standard. Wait...
I've never seen anything
like that before.

MR. SMIT

What?

Clark points to a sophisticated looking
cube that is about the size of a ping-
pong ball.

CLARK

This.

MR. SMIT

The 350s don't have that?

CLARK

No robot has this.

MR. SMIT

What do you think it is?

CLARK

Well, it looks like some
kind of additional brain
circuitry... but with the
way that it's hooked up,
it would override the
entire system.

                    MR. SMIT
Do you think it could be
what's causing the
problem?

                    CLARK
Maybe. Let's pull it and
see what happens.

Clark gentle grabs onto the cube and
tugs on it. It is plugged into the
surrounding hardware and it pulls out
easily.

                    CLARK
Turn it on.

Smit presses the button upon the robot's
chest. The robot sits upright, its
exposed brain lighting up. Its voice is
identical to the P.S.A. 350 that Clark
had repaired earlier.

                THIRD ROBOT
Unit P.S.A. 400-001 ready for task
assignment.

                    MR. SMIT
Well, now that's a lot
better. I mean, now it
sounds like a robot.
Before it sounded

different. It didn't
sound like a robot
should.

Clark eyes the strange cube.

> ### CLARK
> Well, I guess we'll see
> how it does without this.
> Just keep an eye on it
> and give us a call if it
> isn't functioning
> correctly. We can always
> put it back in. — Would
> you mind if I took this
> home to show to my
> father?

> ### MR. SMIT
> If that's the cause of
> the problem as far as I'm
> concerned, you can keep
> it.

> ### CLARK
> Thanks.

EXT. BARNYARD - DAY

Jennifer and Nicholas are laughing,
playing on the hood of a convertible
that is parked in the barnyard behind

the farmhouse. Although slightly
futuristic in design, the car is dented,
beat up, windowless, and its tires are
flat.

Jennifer slides off the hood and runs
past Number 4 who is standing
motionless, watching the children play.
The robots large glass eyes are still
and completely without emotion. Jennifer
eyes the robot as she climbs into the
car's driver seat.

> **JENNIFER**
> Come-on Nicholas, let's
> pretend we're going for a
> drive.

She starts pretending that she is
driving, shifting the gears. Nicholas
climbs down into the passenger seat.

> **NICHOLAS**
> Let's play superhero.

> **JENNIFER**
> Okay, we'll pretend that
> this is the Batmobile.
> I'll be Batman and you
> can be Robin.

NICHOLAS
No, I don't want to be
Robin.

JENNIFER
How come?

NICHOLAS
Because I don't want to.

JENNIFER
Why?

NICHOLAS
Because.

JENNIFER
Because why?

NICHOLAS
Because... Because Robin
is a bird.

Jennifer laughs. Number 4 continues to
silently observe the children,
Jennifer's happy reflection mirrored by
his large glass eyes.

Lisa is watching the children from the
farmhouse's kitchen windows, which
overlook the yard.

INT. KITCHEN - DAY

Lisa's smile deepens as she watches her children play. Andrew steps up behind her. Wrapping his arms around her, he kisses her on the cheek, and then drops his chin down upon her shoulder.

> **LISA**
> I think it's great that you gave them that old car to play with. They're really having a lot of fun with it.

> **ANDREW**
> You know, it's funny, every now and then I wonder if we did the right thing. You know, moving out here from the city, taking over your father's farm... But then when I see how happy the kids are, well, that's when I know that we made the right choice.

EXT. ROAD - DAY

A streamlined postal jeep pulls off the road, parking alongside the mailbox in

front of the Reeves' farmhouse. The
middle aged **MAILMAN** within begins to
sort through a stack of letters.

Breaking, Clark pulls up alongside the
jeep on his bicycle, startling the man.

            MAILMAN
     — Oh, Clark, you scared
    me.

            CLARK
    Sorry, didn't mean to.

Clark and the mailman turn to the sound
of a very loud car that is speeding down
the road toward them. Clark's smile
disappears.

The car screeches to a stop besides the
mail jeep. It is a streamlined, fiery
red convertible, slightly futuristic in
design. Inside the car are **KEVIN**, **TIM**,
and **MARK**, three teenagers. Kevin, a
large boned blonde, a bully and a wise
guy, is driving.

            KEVIN
    Hey Clark, I really dig
    that bike of yours. I bet
    it goes really fast.

Clark glances at the mailman.

                    CLARK
            It gets me where I'm
            going.

The three boys laugh. Kevin elbows the
passenger, Tim.

                    KEVIN
            Ya hear that Tim? It
            get's him where he's
            going. Well, that's
            great, only when you go
            pick up a girl, where
            does she sit? On the
            handlebars?

Kevin's friends laugh louder. Kevin revs
his car's loud engine.

                    KEVIN
            Oh, wait, I forgot. You
            don't date, do you? — Do
            you?

The mailman glances at Clark, whose
nervousness increases.

                    CLARK
            You know... you guys
            think that you're funny,

but you're not.
        (A beat)
Just stupid.

Kevin has been waiting for something like this. He clenches his fists, glaring.

                KEVIN
    What?

                MAILMAN
    — I think you boys should
    leave.

Kevin turns to the mailman, unafraid. The man looks over at Tim and Mark.

                MAILMAN
    Now I know that your
    parents don't want to
    hear about any trouble
    happening out here. I'm
    serious.

After a brief moment:

                TIM
    Come-on Kevin, let's get
    out of here. I don't want
    to waste my day talking
    to Mr. Bicycle. — Mark?

MARK
Yeah, come-on, let's go.

Kevin thinks for a moment and then:

KEVIN
See ya around Clark.

Kevin spins the tires and the car peels off, jetting down the road.

MAILMAN
Don't let those boys get
to you Clark. They're
nothing but trouble.

CLARK
Yeah... I know. It's just
that sometimes they
really burn me up.

The mailman hands Clark a number of letters.

MAILMAN
You just have to let it
go in one ear and out the
other.

Clark forces half a smile.

                    CLARK
          It's not easy when you
          have something between
          your ears.

EXT. FARMHOUSE - DAY

Clark rolls his bike down to the
farmhouse, placing it against a small
fence. Clark's father comes out of the
house.

                    ANDREW
          Clark, back already?

Clark, his mind still on Kevin, hands
the mail to his father.

                    CLARK
          Yeah, it didn't take as
          long as we thought.

                    ANDREW
          So, what was the problem
          out there?

Clark follows his father as he heads
toward the barnyard flipping through the
letters.

CLARK
Oh, nothing big, just
some minor replacements.

He remembers the cube, pulling it out of
his shirt pocket.

CLARK (CONTINUED)
— Oh, and this. I pulled
it out of one of the
robots out there. Never
saw anything like it. It
was plugged into the
brain of a P.S.A. 400.

He hands it to his father as they enter
the barnyard.

ANDREW
A 400?

Jennifer and Nicholas climb out of the
old car and run toward their father.
Number 4 immediately starts to follow
them, watchfully.

SIMULTANEOUS DIALOGUE

CLARK
Yeah, Mr. Smit said that
it was a prototype. What
do you think it is?

JENNIFER
Dad! Dad!

NICHOLAS
Daddy!

END OF SIMULTANEOUS DIALOGUE

Jennifer grabs onto her father. Nicholas moves between his father and Clark.

NICHOLAS
Hi Daddy.

ANDREW
Hey Nicholas.

SIMULTANEOUS DIALOGUE

NICHOLAS
Hi Clark.

JENNIFER
Where ya going Dad?

CLARK
Hi squirt.

ANDREW
Have to give the robots their work assignments honey.

END OF SIMULTANEOUS DIALOGUE

Andrew scoops up Jennifer, carrying her
along as he looks more carefully at
Clark's cube.

> **ANDREW**
> Was it attached directly
> to its memory, hooked
> into all its systems?

> **CLARK**
> Yeah, it was.

> **ANDREW**
> And this P.S.A. was a
> prototype?

> **CLARK**
> That's what he said, an
> "experimental" prototype.

They enter the small barn housing the
other robots.

INT. SMALL BARN - DAY

As they enter, Andrew placed Jennifer
down.

> **ANDREW**
> Hit the lights on the
> left Jennifer.

JENNIFER
Sure thing Dad.

She does so, lighting up the area with
the seated robots. Andrew flicks a
switch on the opposite wall, lighting up
a robot-repair work area, which he moves
to, followed by Clark.

CLARK
So, what do you think it
is?

Andrew examines the cube beneath a
large, lighted, magnifying glass.

ANDREW
I'm not sure but I think
it might be a micro-
cortex. The government
has been playing around
with them for years but
they've never come up
with anything that
actually works.

CLARK
What's it supposed to do?

                    ANDREW
               (Incredulous)
          Well, they're suppose to
          give a robot intellect.

                    CLARK
          The ability to think?

                    ANDREW
          Yep. But they don't work.
          Artificial intelligence
          is just something that's
          beyond our present
          technology.

He tosses the cube to Clark, who catches
it.

                    ANDREW (CONTINUED)
          Someday, in the future,
          they'll find a way to
          give robots the power of
          thought, but believe me,
          it won't be as simple as
          plugging something like
          that into them.

                    CLARK
          So, you don't think it
          can work?

ANDREW
If it worked, Smit
wouldn't have let you
take it.

NICHOLAS
Daddy, what's a smit?

CLARK
Well, can we hook it into
one of ours, just to see
what happens?

ANDREW
It wouldn't be worth the
effort.

Clark is disappointed and it shows.

ANDREW
Clark, it's government.
It would have to be
modified to be installed
and I promised your
mother that I'd do some
things around the house
for her. I wouldn't have
the time.

CLARK
I could do it on my own.

Andrew thinks about it for a moment. He then smiles and wraps an arm around his son.

> **ANDREW**
> All right. Okay. But we can't afford to lose a robot so be careful with it. Understood?

> **CLARK**
> I will. — Which one can I put it into?

Andrew turns to the seated robots. He notices Number 4 standing behind the children.

> **ANDREW**
> Put it in Number 4. I need Number 1 and your mother'll need the others in the orchard today.

> **JENNIFER**
> Dad, can we go to the orchard with Mom? Can we?

> **ANDREW**
> Sure, but leave Number 4 here with Clark, okay?

Jennifer and Nicholas smile.

> **JENNIFER**
> Leave him here? — We
> promise!

EXT. SIDE OF FARMHOUSE - DAY

Robot Number 1 is standing and holding
steady a tall ladder that is leaning
against the side of the farmhouse. It is
looking up toward the roof.

Andrew is standing near the ladder's top
rung. Leaning onto the roof, he is
disconnecting the old weather vane. He
struggles with it for a few moments and
then manages to pull it free. Turning it
about, he looks it over.

> **ANDREW**
> Boy, do you need to be
> cleaned up...

He calls down to the robot.

> **ANDREW**
> Number 1, I'm coming
> down.

Number 1 tightens its grip on the ladder. (The robot's voice is similar to Number 4's.)

> **NUMBER 1**
> I am holding the ladder firmly Mr. Reeves.

Andrew begins to descend the ladder. After taking several steps, the ladder suddenly slides six to eight inches to the right!

> **ANDREW**
> — Number 1! Are you holding the ladder?

Holding the ladder as before, the robot answers, emotionless.

> **NUMBER 1**
> I am holding the ladder firmly Mr. Reeves.

Andrew shakes his head and mumbles to himself as he once again begins to descend.

INT. SMALL BARN - DAY

The other robots are no longer in the barn.

Robot Number 4 is deactivated, sitting lifelessly on a stool in the center of the repair area. The robot's transparent head cap has been removed and Clark is hard at work installing Smit's cube.

> **CLARK**
> This is tricky…

Clark picks up a soldering tool and digs back into Number 4's head.

> **CLARK**
> Clark Reeves... Brain surgeon.

Slumped forward, the robot's metal face is lifeless, its large glass eyes dark and empty.

After a time, Clark slowly pulls his hands out of Number 4's head and cracks an uncertain smile.

> **CLARK**
> Well Number 4, that does it. I think.

Clark takes one last peek inside the robot's head and then steps around to the front of the robot.

                    CLARK (CONTINUED)
          Now all we have to do is
          turn you on and hope that
          your system doesn't shut
          down.

Clark looks at the button in the center
of the robot's chest. He does not reach
out for it right away.

                    CLARK
          I hope I did this right.

He pushes in the button. There is a
click and the robot's brain lights up.
At once sparks of electricity flash and
crackle. Clark jumps back a step.

                    CLARK
          Oh no...

The sparks suddenly stop and the robot
lifts it head, looking to Clark. The
robot's voice sounds slightly different,
as if it has a trace of emotion in it.

                    NUMBER 4
          Good afternoon Clark. Today is
          Thursday, July the eleventh, the
          one hundred and ninety...

The robot's speech slows. Number 4
suddenly appears slightly confused.
Turning left to right, the robot
examines its surroundings with its glass
eyes.

> **NUMBER 4** (CONTINUED)
> se... cond... day of... this... year...

The robot turns back to Clark, its
speech returning to normal for a brief
moment.

> **NUMBER 4** (CONTINUED)
> There are one hundred and
> seventy three...

Number 4 starts to look around again.

> **NUMBER 4** (CONTINUED)
> days... remaining...

> **CLARK**
> I knew it, something's
> wrong.

Clark peeks inside the robot's head. Its
brain is alive with dancing lights. The
cube that he installed is glowing. Clark
taps the cube with a screwdriver and
receiving a shock he jumps back.

> **NUMBER 4**
> It is four thirty two pm. Where are
> Jennifer and Nicholas?

> **CLARK**
> Picking apples in the
> orchard.

Number 4 tilts its head, staring, in an
odd way, at the light hanging above it.

> **NUMBER 4**
> Should I be there?... With the
> children?

Clark stares at the robot for a moment
before answering, suspecting that
whatever is different may not
necessarily be wrong.

> **CLARK**
> Let me put your brain cap
> on and we'll go down to
> the orchard together.

Number 4 is still staring up at the
light. The light's reflection fills the
robot's round, glass eyes with a warm
glow.

> **NUMBER 4**
> ... We will go down to the orchard
> together...

Empty Eyes

Niko Zinovii

Act Two

Niko Zinovii

EXT. FARM - DAY

The orchard of fruit trees lies beneath the large hexagonal glass plates of an enormous, dome shaped greenhouse.

INT. ORCHARD GREENHOUSE - DAY

The orchard's fruit trees stand in neat, orderly rows. Robots number 2, 3, 5, and 6 are dispersed through the greenhouse. Standing on stepladders, the robots are picking fruit and placing it into wooden baskets.

Lisa is moving from tree to tree, turning on faucets that empty water upon the ground surrounding the trunks of the trees.

Jennifer and Nicholas are half way up an apple tree, laughing, struggling to climb higher.

> **LISA**
> Jennifer — Nicholas! How many times do I have to tell you that I don't want you climbing the trees?

She moves to the children, a bit tired
and frustrated.

> JENNIFER
> Can't we just climb this
> one tree? Please.

> LISA
> Jennifer.

> JENNIFER
> We won't knock any apples
> off. I promise.

> NICHOLAS
> Yeah Mom, we promise.

> JENNIFER
> Didn't you ever climb a
> tree when you were a kid?

> LISA
> Yes but —

> JENNIFER
> — Apple trees?

Lisa smiles.

> LISA
> Yes, especially apple
> tree.

(A beat)
I used to drive your
grandmother crazy.

NICHOLAS
Mom, are we driving you
crazy?

LISA
Honey, with all the work
I have to do today I
really don't think it's a
drive, it's more like a
short walk.

CLARK (O.S.)
Mom.

They turn to see Clark entering the
domed orchard with Number 4.

CLARK (CONTINUED)
I brought Number 4 out to
watch the kids.

LISA
And not a moment too
soon.

Nicholas turns to Jennifer, whispering,
as Clark walks Number 4 over to Lisa.

NICHOLAS
He's back. Why's he
always following us?

JENNIFER
Because that's what Mom
programmed him to do.
It's what she wants.
That's why Mom and Dad
made him.

NICHOLAS
Made him?

Clark and the robot stop in front of
Lisa. Number 4 continues to act a bit
odd, unusually aware of and interested
in its surroundings.

CLARK
Just keep an eye on him,
he's acting a little
strange.

LISA
Is something wrong with
him?

CLARK
I don't know yet. I put
something into his —

NUMBER 4
Jennifer, Nicholas, you must come
down from that tree immediately.
(Eyes wander off)
You... are not allowed up there...

LISA
It's all right Number 4.
They can climb trees
today.

Number 4 is slightly confused.

Laughing, Jennifer sticks her tongue out
at the robot. Surprisingly, Number 4
displays a slight reaction to this and
takes a step back. Jennifer did not
expect the robot to react and she is
surprised. Number 4 does not take its
eyes off her.

JENNIFER
Stop it. — Stop looking
at me. — Stop it.

LISA
Jennifer, what's wrong?

JENNIFER
I don't like the way he's
staring at us with those
empty eyes.

Number 4 displays a puzzled reaction to her description of its eyes.

> **LISA**
> Honey, he's only a robot.

Number 4 becomes slightly disturbed.

Lisa does not know what to make of this and turns to Clark who shrugs. There is a brief moment of silence as Lisa eyes the robot.

> **NICHOLAS**
> Mom, where did Number 4
> come from? Jennifer says
> that you and Daddy made
> him. Did you make him
> like you made us?

Lisa smiles as Number 4 turns to her, awaiting her answer.

> **LISA**
> No honey, that's all
> together different.

> **NICHOLAS**
> But Daddy said that
> little girls were made of
> sugar and spice and
> everything that's nice.

The robot is listening to every word, following the conversation.

> **LISA**
> And that little boys were made of frogs and snails and little puppy dog tails?

> **NICHOLAS**
> Yeah, so what's Number 4 made of? He looks like he's made of toasters and spoons and nails.

Clark watches as the robot swings its eyes to Lisa, awaiting her response.

> **LISA**
> Nicholas, your father was just teasing you about the puppy dog tails. Both you and your sister came from the love that your father and I share.

> **JENNIFER**
> Yeah, we came from inside her stomach.

> **NICHOLAS**
> Inside? Number 4 too?

> **JENNIFER**
> No silly, he came from...

She looks down at Number 4. The robot's eyes meet hers.

> **JENNIFER**
> He came from out of a
> box.

> **NICHOLAS**
> Huh?

Jennifer and Number 4's eyes are still locked.

> **LISA**
> I'll explain it all to
> you later Nicholas, but
> right now, I've got to
> get back to work.

She turns to Number 4, noticing that the robot is still looking up at Jennifer.

> **LISA** (CONTINUED)
> Number 4, you can start
> picking ripe apples off
> this tree.

Number 4 does not respond.

> **LISA**
> Number 4?

The robot turns to her, its computerized
mind is elsewhere.

> **NUMBER 4**
> I will pick the ripe apples off this
> tree.

> **LISA**
> Good.
> (To Clark)
> There really is something
> wrong with him. Could it
> be the heat?

> **CLARK**
> No, it's not the heat.

> **LISA**
> Well, I just hope it's
> not serious.

She walks off, heading back to the water
faucets.

Number 4 picks up a wooden basket and
steps up to several large red apples
that are hanging from the tree. Glancing
up at Jennifer, Number 4 then looks off
at the other robots working in the

orchard. The robot then glances off at Lisa and back at Clark.

CLARK
Go on, pick the apples.

Slowly, Number 4 reaches out to pick an apple of the tree. The robot freezes as it hears Jennifer say:

JENNIFER
Empty Eyes...

Number 4 thinks for a moment. His eyes then lower, unsure, and he picks the apple off the tree, imbued by self-awareness and living consciousness.

EXT. SIDE OF FARMHOUSE - DUSK

The sun is setting. Andrew is climbing up the ladder, carrying the weather vane back up to the roof. He drops it down on its base. It is now clean and shiny, like new. A breeze spins it about, turning its large eyed face to Andrew, who smiles at his work.

Andrew starts down the ladder.

EXT. BARNYARD - DUSK

Clark exits the farmhouse and moves to the small barn that houses the robots.

INT. SMALL BARN - DUSK

All six robots are sitting on their bench in numerical order. They are alert, sitting upright and staring straight ahead, except for Number 4 who is looking at the robot repair area. Clark enters.

> **CLARK**
> Bed time guys.

Clark presses the button on robot number 1's chest. Immediately, the robot slumps forward and becomes lifeless. Number 4 reacts to this, frightened. Clark turns off robot number 2, followed by robot number 3. He then prepares to do the same to Number 4.

> **NUMBER 4**
> — Clark...

Clark stops short of pressing Number 4's chest button.

> **CLARK**
> I was wondering when you were going to start talking again. Why were you silent all evening? After I left you in the orchard?

The robot does not answer.

> **CLARK**
> Number 4?

> **NUMBER 4**
> I do not know.
>   (A beat)
> Clark...

> **CLARK**
> Yes?

Number 4 glances at the robots to his right that have been turned off.

> **NUMBER 4**
> Why do you turn us off at the end of the day?

> **CLARK**
> Why? To conserve your battery. That way we don't have to recharge

you every day.

Clark notices how Number 4 is listening
to him, as if the robot were human.
Number 4's voice seems to contain more
emotion now.

> **CLARK**
> Number 4, your question
> has nothing to do with
> your programming. Why did
> you ask it?

> **NUMBER 4**
> I am not sure.

> **CLARK**
> Was it because you were
> thinking about it? About
> being turned off?

> **NUMBER 4**
> Thinking about it...
> (A beat)
> I am not sure.

> **CLARK**
> Number 4... I attached a
> micro-cortex to your
> brain this morning. It's
> supposed to give you the
> ability to reason. To

think. Now, I don't know
if it's working or not,
but if it is, then you're
going to be different.
You're not going to be
like these other robots
anymore.

Number 4 leans forward, looking at the
two robots on his left. Facing forward,
they are displaying no interest in their
conversation or in anything.

NUMBER 4
Clark, your father, Mr. Reeves, he
made me and the others. That is
how I came to be, is it not?

Clark turns off robots number 5 and 6.

CLARK
Well, yeah. He didn't
like any of the models on
the market so he ordered
away for different parts
and he built you. And the
others.

Number 4 grows more disturbed.

CLARK
Does that bother you?

Number 4 thinks for a moment before answering.

> **NUMBER 4**
> No.
> (A beat)
> I am ready to be turned off now.

Clark stares into Number 4's round glass eyes. He then slowly reaches forward and places his finger on the robot's chest button.

> **CLARK**
> Good night Number 4.

> **NUMBER 4**
> Good night Clark.

Clark pushes in the button. It clicks and there is darkness.

THERE ARE SEVERAL MOMENTS OF SILENT DARKNESS AND THEN:

INT. SMALL BARN - DAY

Click. Jennifer is pulling her finger away from the on/off button on Number 4's chest plate. Nicholas is standing alongside her. Both the children are unhappy about turning on the robot who is sitting alone on the bench.

As he comes to life, Number 4 purposely avoids eye contact with Jennifer.

> **NUMBER 4**
> Good afternoon Jennifer and Nicholas. Today is Saturday, Jul —
> (A beat)
> Why was I not turned on, on Friday?

The children look at each other, surprised.

> **NUMBER 4**
> Why?

Jennifer does not really want to answer the robot but does.

> **JENNIFER**
> We all went to Aunt Joan's yesterday.

> **NUMBER 4**
> Yesterday... Friday is now yesterday. Friday was to be tomorrow when I was turned off.

> **NICHOLAS**
> How come he sounds different?

Jennifer shrugs.

> **NUMBER 4**
> Did Mrs. Reeves instruct you to
> turn me on?

> **JENNIFER**
> Yes, my mother wants us
> to bring you with us.

> **NUMBER 4**
> Where are you going?

> **JENNIFER**
> To the cow barn. The
> corn's getting high so me
> and Nicholas are going to
> make a scarecrow for the
> field.

Number 4 rises, looking about.

> **NUMBER 4**
> Jennifer, where are the other
> robots. Where is Mr. Reeves?
> Where is Clark?

> **JENNIFER**
> They —
> (A beat)
> "Mr. Reeves" and Clark
> had to take the other

robots away. They started
acting mean so my
father's going to have
them melted.

NUMBER 4
They were taken away? To be
melted?

JENNIFER
That's right. So if you
don't want to get melted
too you'd better start
acting nicer. Especially
to me and Nicholas. Now,
come-on.

Jennifer turns her back to the robot and
smiles devilishly, leading Nicholas out
into the barnyard.

Number 4 is absolutely motionless for a
moment and then he quickly starts to
follow the children.

EXT. BARNYARD - DAY

Number 4 follows the children, looking
about nervously.

NUMBER 4
Melted...

Jennifer and Nicholas start to laugh, silently.

After several moments, the robot stops dead in its tracks. On the side of the farmhouse, working under Lisa's supervision, are the five missing robots. They are painting the Reeves home.

NUMBER 4
Melted?

Number 4 sees the children disappear into a large red barn. The robot sets after them, takes long, stiff, purposeful strides.

NUMBER 4
Jennifer.

INT. LARGE BARN - DAY

Laughing, the children run past the stalled cows and leap onto a mound of straw in the back of the barn. Number 4 enters, heading for the children.

NICHOLAS
Here he comes.

The robot reaches them.

NUMBER 4
Jennifer... Mr. Reeves did not take
the others away to have them
melted. You lied.

JENNIFER
That was to get you back
for always tellin' on us
and getting us in
trouble.

NUMBER 4
I do not understand.

JENNIFER
Oh yes you do. You
thought that you were in
trouble. That my Dad was
going to melt you. Now
you know how it feels to
be in trouble. Just
givin' you some of your
own medicine.
        (To Nicholas)
Come-on Nicholas, let's
start stuffin' some of
those old clothes.

She pulls Nicholas toward a pile of old
clothes. Number 4 is silent, following
their movements with his large round
eyes.

NUMBER 4

Jennifer.

JENNIFER

What? Are you going to
tell on me now for lying?

NUMBER 4

No.
   (A beat)
Telling on you and placing you in
trouble... it was never something
that I did intentionally. I never
meant to make you feel
frightened. I was only following my
programming... I am sorry.

The children are dumbfounded.

NICHOLAS

What did he say?

JENNIFER

He apologized...

NUMBER 4

I now understand why you dislike
me. Why you call me names...
and try to hurt me with words.
So... do not worry... I will not place
you in trouble anymore. I will not
look at you with my... "Empty

Eyes"... and I will not bother your
ears with the sound of my
movements.
(A beat)
Good-bye.

Number 4 starts off, accidentally
stepping on the end of a rake lying on
the ground. Flashing up, the rake hits
the robot square in the face.

NUMBER 4
— Oh.

Number 4 stumbles backward, his arms
swinging about, attempting to balance
himself. He bangs into the cow stall
behind him. The cow within moos as a
large milking pail falls off the shelf
above the robot. The pail clangs as it
drops onto and covers Number 4's head.
Number 4 falls into a seated position,
landing upon a pile of cow manure. His
voice echoes within the pail.

NUMBER 4
Who? — What? — I cannot see.

The children burst out laughing. Number
4 finally manages to lift the pail off
his head.

NUMBER 4
I am sitting upon cow excrement.

The children laugh so hard their stomachs hurt. The robot turns to the children, observing them. Their laughing reflection is mirrored by his glass eyes. An important moment passes and then, unexpectedly, the robot starts to laugh. Never having laughed before, his laugh is slow and unsure.

Startled, the children become silent. Number 4 quickly silences himself. There is absolute silence as the children and the robot stare at each other.

Suddenly, the cow housed in the stall behind the robot defecates right upon the robot's head. Number 4 starts to laugh and the children immediately join him.

EXT. BARNYARD - DAY

The laughter is heard across the barnyard. Several moments pass.

EXT. BACK OF RED BARN - DAY

Number 4 is standing in an awkward, bent over position. Spraying a hose, Jennifer

is washing the cow manure off the robot.
Nicholas is watching.

JENNIFER
There, you're all clean.

NUMBER 4
Nicholas, has all of the excrement
been washed off my head?

Nicholas laughs.

NICHOLAS
You're funny.

JENNIFER
Don't worry, you're
clean.

She turns the water off.

JENNIFER
Do you want to help us
make our scarecrow?

NUMBER 4
You, you want me to help you?

JENNIFER
Yeah, it'll be fun.

> **NUMBER 4**
> But, I have never made a
> scarecrow before.

> **JENNIFER**
> It's easy, we'll show you
> how.

INT. LARGE BARN - DAY

Jennifer and Nicholas lead Number 4 into
the cow barn. The robot glances
disapprovingly at the cow that had
defecated on him.

Jennifer grabs an old pair of jeans and
begins stuffing it with straw.

> **JENNIFER**
> See, it's simple. All you
> have to do is stuff the
> clothes with straw.
> Nicholas, why don't you
> get a shirt and —

Jennifer stops in mid sentence, looking
at Number 4.

> **JENNIFER**
> You know, I just
> realized... You're not
> wearing any clothes.

Number 4 looks over his metallic body, confused and a bit embarrassed.

> **NICHOLAS**
> Yeah, you're bare.

> **NUMBER 4**
> Robots do not wear clothes.

> **JENNIFER**
> But even the scarecrow
> that we're makin' is
> going to have clothes.
> Right Nicholas?

> **NICHOLAS**
> Yeah.

> **NUMBER 4**
> But... Robots do not wear clothes.

> **JENNIFER**
> If men made out of straw
> wear clothes then men
> made out of metal should
> be able to wear clothes
> too.

> **NICHOLAS**
> Yeah.

Number 4 looks at Nicholas and then at Jennifer.

NUMBER 4
Yes. You are correct.

EXT. FARMHOUSE AND SURROUNDINGS - DAY

A streamlined station wagon turns off the road in front of the farmhouse and rolls down the home's short gravel driveway. Andrew is driving, Clark is riding passenger. A deactivated, **TALL ROBOT** is lying in the back of the wagon.

Lisa, still supervising the robots that are painting the house, smiles and moves to the car. She gives Andrew a hug and a fast kiss as Clark moves to the back of the car.

LISA
I forgot that you were leaving early to go out to Carl's. I missed having coffee with you.

ANDREW
Well, we'll just have to have coffee together tonight.

                    LISA
        Is that a promise?

                  ANDREW
        You have my word.

                CLARK (O.S.)
        Dad.

Andrew and Lisa move to the back of the
car. Clark is pulling out the robot. The
robot is metallic blue and red with an
alphanumeric identification, "R.A. -
1500 - 2651" printed across it s chest.
Its head is large and round.

                  ANDREW
        What's the hurry Clark?

                   CLARK
        Oh, I'm just anxious to
        check on Number 4.
        Haven't been able to see
        him since Thursday.

Andrew helps Clark. The robot is heavy
and it is difficult. As they pull:

                  ANDREW
        Still hoping that cube is
        going to work?

                    CLARK
          Well, he did start to act
          kind of strange.

Andrew reacts.

                    CLARK
          — Oh, he's not
          malfunctioning or
          anything. He was just
          asking questions and... I
          don't know, he seemed
          unusually aware and
          interested in his
          surroundings.

They drop the blue and red robot down
upon its feet, straightening it into a
standing position. It is over six and a
half feet tall.

                    LISA
          Oh, he's tall. Japanese?

Andrew nods yes.

                    LISA
          Carl would buy foreign.

                    CLARK
          Mom, where's Number 4?

LISA
I have him watching
Jennifer and Nicholas.
Oh, there they go.

In the distance: The children and Number
4 are walking across the barnyard,
carrying a scarecrow. The robot is
dressed in a pair of farmer jeans with
suspenders.

LISA (CONTINUED)
Oh, isn't that adorable.
They dressed him up. Put
pants on him.

CLARK
They look like they're
having fun with him. Kind
of strange, isn't it? I
mean the way they're
always complaining about
him.
LISA
That is kind of odd.

CLARK
Dad... How do we know it
wasn't Number 4's idea to
put on those pants?

Andrew looks off at the robot.

LISA
What's this about, that
micro-cortex thing you
told me about?

ANDREW
Yep.

LISA
You don't think it works,
do you?

ANDREW
I don't know.
(To Clark)
Bring him up to the house
later, I'll take a look
at him.

EXT. CORN FIELD - DAY

From a distance: The children and Number
4 leave the barnyard, carrying the
scarecrow into a nearby cornfield. They
are talking and having fun.

They hang the scarecrow up on a tall
wooden post located in the center of the
field. Stepping back, the three of them
stare up at the man of straw, admiring
what they have made.

<u>Close</u>: Nicholas takes a hold of the robot's right hand. Number 4 looks at the boy, surprised. A moment passes. Number 4 slowly reaches down with his free hand and takes one of Jennifer's hands. She smiles at him. Slowly, Number 4 turns back to the scarecrow. Its human-like reflection is mirrored by his large, round, glass eyes.

EXT. FARMHOUSE - DUSK

The lights are on throughout the first floor of the home.

INT. KITCHEN - DUSK

Lisa is struggling to open a large bag of puppy chow, trying to avoid stepping on the puppies crawling about beneath her feet. Cleopatra, sitting nearby, barks impatiently.

> **LISA**
> Just a second Cleo.

Jennifer and Nicholas are standing in the adjacent hallway, taking turns peeking through the keyhole of a closed door.

Lisa tears open the bag and dog food
accidentally spills out onto the floor.
The puppies attack the food.

> **LISA**
> Jennifer, can you give me
> a hand?

> **JENNIFER**
> Right now?

> **LISA**
> Yes, now.

Upset, Jennifer stomps into the kitchen,
letting Nicholas have the keyhole all to
himself.

> **LISA**
> I tell you Jennifer, I
> don't understand you two.
> Everyday you're telling
> me that I don't let you
> spend

NICHOLAS'S P.O.V.: Nicholas can see his
father and Clark examining Number 4 who
is seated in the center of the room.
Number 4's transparent head cap has been
removed and Andrew is looking at the
robot's brain.

           LISA (O.S. CONTINUED)
    enough time with the
    puppies and now I bring
    them in the house for the
    first time and you ignore
    them.

BACK TO:

           JENNIFER
    Mom, is Number 4 in
    trouble?

           LISA
    No, honey, your father
    just wants to talk to
    him.

Jennifer does not believe this.

INT. DEN - DUSK

Andrew is examining the installed micro-cortex.

           ANDREW
    So, you attached it
    directly to the memory?

Number 4 is uncomfortable. He looks from Andrew to Clark.

CLARK
Well, I tried to at first
but I just couldn't get
it linked to the rest of
the brain that way so...
I kind of combined the
memory box and the micro-
cortex, making them one
unit. It was the only way
that I could get it to
work.

ANDREW
So, now it's impossible
to remove it without
taking apart the entire
brain. — And it's now
inseparable from the
memory unit. To separate
them you'd probably
damage both in the
process.

CLARK
Sorry, I guess I should
have asked you first. But
it is working. Isn't it?

Andrew sits down. Number 4's eyes follow
him.

ANDREW

Yes, it certainly is. And
that gives us a problem.
Doesn't it?

CLARK

A problem?

ANDREW

Clark, this mirco-cortex,
it's something very
different, radical. It's
not that you improved a
robot's ability to walk
or you increased the
dexterity of its hands.
Modifying and attaching
that cortex the way you
did, you gave this
"machine" intelligence.
Conscious thought. It's
alive now.

Number 4 is listening intently.

CLARK

I don't understand. You
sound like you think
there's something wrong
with what I did. Like you
don't think it's right.

ANDREW

No, I think that this is
incredible and as a
scientist I welcome it
but...
    (A beat)
But I don't think that
the world is ready for
this. Not yet. This is
far ahead of its time.

CLARK

So?

ANDREW

Well, giving the world a
thinking but "soulless"
robot will prompt people
to re-examine their own
place in life. Some of
them might wonder whether
or not man is little more
than a thinking, soulless
animal. This is
disturbing. People won't
accept the robot.

NUMBER 4

Mr. Reeves, I am confused.
    (A beat)
I know that I am a "machine"
but... I am not a man made out of

straw. I feel alive. I do not feel empty inside. If men like you have souls then I should have a soul too. Is this not correct?

CLARK
You don't understand Number 4.

NUMBER 4
Robots do not have souls?

CLARK
I didn't say that, I meant that you didn't understand what my father meant. Look, you're different now and because you're different people aren't going to want to accept you. Understand?

NUMBER 4
No. Not yet.

ANDREW
Clark, I think that for now we should keep this to ourselves. Until we feel it's the right time to make it public. It'll give us time to gather

documentation, analyze
this; study what you've
created.

Clark does not answer.

> **ANDREW**
> Clark?

> **CLARK**
> Yeah, I guess your right.

> **ANDREW**
> Good. Number 4, why don't
> you go out to the barn.
> Clark will come out in a
> little while and turn you
> off.

Number 4 looks at his brain cap.

> **NUMBER 4**
> My brain cap is not attached.

> **ANDREW**
> That's okay, you can take
> it with you. Clark will
> put it on later.

Number 4 is disturbed. He is silent for
a moment.

> **NUMBER 4**
> I will go to the barn.

INT. HALL AND KITCHEN - DUSK

Nicholas moves away from the keyhole as the door opens and Number 4 steps out of the den.

> **NICHOLAS**
> You okay?

> **NUMBER 4**
> I am not sure Nicholas.

Carrying his brain cap, Number 4 walks past Nicholas and into the kitchen. The robot is embarrassed that his brain cap is not connected to his head. Jennifer notices this.

> **JENNIFER**
> Number 4, do you want to
> play with the puppies?

> **NUMBER 4**
> I cannot. Mr. Reeves instructed
> me to go to the barn... and wait
> for Clark to turn me off.
> (A beat)
> I hope he will turn me on
> tomorrow. On Sunday.

JENNIFER
(Whispers)
Don't worry, I will.

NUMBER 4
Goodnight Jennifer.

JENNIFER
Goodnight Number 4.

Number 4 walks through the kitchen,
heading toward the back door. Lisa
leaves, entering the den. She closes the
door behind her.

NICHOLAS
Goodnight Number 4.

Number 4 does not turn around.

NUMBER 4
Goodnight Nicholas.

NICHOLAS
(To Jennifer)
Why's Daddy makin' him go
outside without the top
of his head on?

Jennifer looks at the den's closed door.

> **JENNIFER**
> I guess Dad's punishing
> him for not acting like
> he's supposed to. He's
> not supposed to have fun
> with us you know. Mom and
> Dad only want him to
> order us around.

> **NICHOLAS**
> He got in trouble because
> he played with us?

> **JENNIFER**
> Yep. It's our fault.

EXT. BARNYARD - NIGHT

Number 4 is walking toward the small
barn. Despite the moon growing brighter
and the sound of chirping crickets, a
lonely atmosphere prevails.

Number 4 looks off to the cornfield. He
sees the scarecrow that he helped the
children create. It is hanging high
above the field, heavily shadowed, and
completely alone. Number 4 shudders ever
so slightly and then enters the small
barn.

INT. SMALL BARN - NIGHT

Number 4 steps in front of the five
robots that are sitting silently upon
the long bench. They are all staring
straight ahead, paying no attention to
him. Number 4 stares at these robots for
a moment.

Number 4 then remembers that he is
carrying his transparent brain cap. He
moves toward the robot repair area. The
Japanese robot is lying down upon the
large table in that area. It is still
deactivated and its torso has been
separated from its legs. Number 4 slows
his approach, gazing at the dismembered
robot. He notices that the robot's hands
have been removed and are lying together
on the table, separated from its body.

Number 4 slowly places his brain cap
down upon the table. He sees that the
insides of the Japanese robot have been
removed and that its torso is hollow.
Number 4 becomes disturbed. He backs
away from the table.

Turning about, Number 4 comes face to
face with a mirror on the wall. He steps
closer to it, looking into his own eyes.
He raises a trembling hand and touches

his right cheek.

>   **NUMBER 4**
>   ... Empty eyes...

>   **CLARK** (O.S.)
>   Number 4.

Number 4 spins about to face Clark who
is standing before the seated robots.

>   **CLARK**
>   ... I'll just turn the
>   others off and then we
>   can put your brain cap
>   back on.

Clark turns them off, one after the
other. Number 4 walks over to him.

>   **NUMBER 4**
>   Clark.

>   **CLARK**
>   Yeah?

Number 4 holds out his metal, skeleton-
like hands.

>   **NUMBER 4**
>   I know that I am made out of...
>   parts. My hands, my limbs, my

brain cap... They are parts of me.

He looks over to his brain cap.

> **NUMBER 4** (CONTINUED)
> But... seeing something separated
> from me... It makes me feel that I
> am empty inside. That I am not
> important.

Clark quickly moves to the worktable.

> **CLARK**
> I'm sorry, I didn't
> realize how you must
> feel.

Clark begins to reattach the robot's
brain cap.

> **NUMBER 4**
> Clark.

> **CLARK**
> Yes.

> **NUMBER 4**
> Please do not turn me off tonight.
> It frightens me.

CLARK
It shouldn't frighten
you. There's nothing to
worry about.

NUMBER 4
I cannot help... "thinking"... what if
you do not turn me on tomorrow.
What if I am never turned back
on.

The brain cap is secured. Clark steps in
front of the robot, facing him.

CLARK
But I have to recharge
your battery.

NUMBER 4
Please do not turn me off.

Clark thinks for a moment.

CLARK
Okay. I won't turn you
off.
      (A beat)
But robot's don't sleep
you know, you'll only be
sitting there all night,
staring at the walls.

NUMBER 4
I will stare at the walls.

Clark smiles.

CLARK
Okay, come-on over to the
bench and let me plug you
in.

NUMBER 4
Thank you Clark.

EXT. FARMHOUSE - NIGHT

The farmhouse is dark.

EXT. BARNYARD - NIGHT

The barnyard is dark and empty.
Somewhere O.S. an owl hoots.

EXT. SKY - NIGHT

A drifting cloud passes in front of the
moon.

INT. SMALL BARN - NIGHT

Number 4 is sitting, in numerical order,
amongst the other robots. One of his
pant legs is rolled up to his knee and a

large electrical plug is attached to his
calf. The lights from his working brain
are dancing beneath his brain cap and he
is staring at the wall in front of him.

EXT. FARMHOUSE - NIGHT

A breeze blows. The polished weather
vane on the roof turns in the wind.

INT. PARENT'S BEDROOM -NIGHT

Andrew and Lisa are both sound asleep.
The clock on Lisa's night table reads:
1:02

INT. CHILDREN'S BEDROOM - NIGHT

Both children are awake and dressed.
Jennifer is tying Nicholas's shoes. She
whispers:

> **JENNIFER**
> Okay, let's go.

INT. HALL OUTSIDE BEDROOMS - NIGHT

The children sneak out into the hall,
tip toeing by their parent's bedroom.

EXT. BARNYARD - NIGHT

Jennifer leads Nicholas toward the small barn housing the robots.

INT. SMALL BARN - NIGHT

Number 4 is staring at the moths flapping about the room's hanging light. The children enter.

> **JENNIFER**
> Number 4, we came to visit you.

> **NICHOLAS**
> Yeah.

The robot is surprised.

> **JENNIFER**
> (To Nicholas)
> See, I told you Clark would put his head back together.

> **NUMBER 4**
> Jennifer, Nicholas, why are you here? Why are you not sleeping?

JENNIFER
I already told you, we
came to visit you.

NUMBER 4
Visit me? Why?

JENNIFER
Because we were worried
about you.

NUMBER 4
You were worried about me?

JENNIFER
Yeah, you always worry
about friends when
they're in trouble.

NUMBER 4
Friends?
(A beat)
Are you my friends?

JENNIFER
Of course we are, silly.

NICHOLAS
Of course, silly.

Number 4 is at a loss for words. There
is a moment of silence.

JENNIFER
It's quiet out here. You
must be lonely. And
bored.

Number 4 does not quite understand.

JENNIFER
Hey... It's a long time
'till morning, why don't
we go have some fun.

NICHOLAS
Yeah, let's go play.

NUMBER 4
Play? What would we do?

JENNIFER
Well...
        (A beat)
We could collect
treasure.

NUMBER 4
Collect treasure?

JENNIFER
Yeah, Nicholas and me
have a whole box full.
Don't we Nicholas?

NICHOLAS
Yeah, in the cow barn. Do
you want to see it?

Before Number 4 can answer, Jennifer
unplugs him.

JENNIFER
Of course he does.

She takes the robot by the hand.

JENNIFER (CONTINUED)
Come-on Number 4.

EXT. BARNYARD - NIGHT

Jennifer and Nicholas, each holding one
of the robot's hands, pull him across
the barnyard. Number 4 struggles to keep
up with them, taking short, quick,
mechanical strides. The squeaking of
Number 4's knees no longer bothers
Nicholas.

INT. LARGE BARN - NIGHT

The children giggle as they pull him
into the cow barn. Several cows awake,
mooing. Jennifer steps over to a ladder
that leads up to a hayloft.

                    JENNIFER
Come-on.

She starts up the ladder.

                    NICHOLAS
The treasure's up there.

Nicholas follows Jennifer and Number 4
follows Nicholas.

INT. HAY LOFT - NIGHT

The children steps off the ladder,
moving into the darkness. As Number 4's
head pops up from below, the light
emanating from his brain brightens the
area.

Jennifer moves back to a wall, looking
for and finding a dark hole in the wood.
Nicholas and Number 4 push through the
straw, moving up behind her.

                    JENNIFER
        There, see that hole,
        it's in there. Our
        treasure's in there. And
        it's real, real safe.

                    NUMBER 4
        I do not understand.

Jennifer and Nicholas exchange smiling, knowing nods.

> **JENNIFER**
> Reach in there and pull
> out the treasure.

> **NUMBER 4**
> In the hole?

Jennifer grins and nods 'yes' and Nicholas smiles widely.

> **JENNIFER**
> Go on. Don't be scared.

Number 4 hesitates and then cautiously reaches forward, slowly inserting a skeleton-like hand into the dark hole. The hole is deep and the robot's forearm slowly disappears.

> **NUMBER 4**
> I think I —

Suddenly there is a loud SNAP! Number 4 yanks his arm out of the hole, pulling his hand into the light being given off by his electrical brain. There is a large mouse trap snapped closed on his metal fingers. The children laugh loudly.

NUMBER 4
I understand now.

Number 4 removes the trap as Jennifer
pulls an old cigar box from the hole.
They all kneel around the box.

JENNIFER
Okay... Are you ready?

Number 4 stares at the box in
anticipation.
NUMBER 4
— Yes.

Jennifer slowly opens the box. Number 4
stares silently at its contents, in awe.
The box is filled with a child's
treasure: Several colorful marbles, a
large sea shell, the circular bottom of
a broken soda bottle, a small rubber
monster, several links of a bicycle
chain, different colored bird feathers,
a small marble floor tile, etc.

NUMBER 4
... This is your treasure...

Number 4 picks up one of the feathers,
holding it before his large, glass eyes.
It is blue and beautiful. He slowly
twists it about, appreciating it.

NUMBER 4
It is strange how things appear
different now. Their shapes and
colors hold a new meaning.

NICHOLAS
Look at this one.

Nicholas hands the robot a large orange
marble. Number 4 stares at it,
appreciating a beauty that most do not
see.

NUMBER 4
It is made of glass... So round...
and orange. The color is warm.
(To Jennifer)
Is that description accurate?

JENNIFER
Yes, orange is warm, blue
is cold. — What about
this one. This one's my
favorite.

She places the seashell against the
robot's ear hole.

JENNIFER (CONTINUED)
Listen to it.

Number 4 listens, silently.

> **NUMBER 4**
> What is that sound? I have never
> heard it before.

> **JENNIFER**
> That's what the ocean
> sounds like.

Number 4 takes the shell from Jennifer,
keeping it pressed against the side of
his head.

> **NICHOLAS**
> He likes it.

> **JENNIFER**
> Do you want to see the
> rest?

> **NUMBER 4**
> — Yes. I want to see all of the
> treasure.

EXT. BARNYARD - NIGHT

The cow barn is bathed by the warm glow
of the moon. The crickets are chirping a
peaceful, pleasant melody.

> **DISSOLVE TO:**

EXT. BARNYARD - DAWN

The cow barn is brightened by the rays
of the rising sun. The farm's rooster
cries out somewhere O.S.

INT. KITCHEN - DAY

Clark, Jennifer, and Nicholas are
sitting around the breakfast table. Lisa
is at the stove. Jennifer and Nicholas
are exhausted, half asleep at the table.
Lisa reaches for Nicholas's cereal bowl.

> **LISA**
> Are you done with this?

Nicholas manages to nod 'yes.' Lisa
moves to the sink with the bowl.

> **LISA**
> Why are you two so tired
> this morning? You look
> like you didn't sleep a
> wink.

Jennifer and Nicholas exchange a secret
grin.

INT. HALL OUTSIDE BEDROOMS - DAY

Lisa steps out of her bedroom,

straightening her Sunday dress, rushing.
She pokes her head into the children's
room.

INT. CHILDREN'S BEDROOM - DAY

Jennifer and Nicholas are dressing.
Jennifer is helping her brother.

>   **LISA**
> You two almost ready?

>   **NICHOLAS**
> Almost.

>   **LISA**
> Good, mass starts in
> fifteen minutes. Where's
> Clark?

Jennifer smiles.

>   **JENNIFER**
> He went to get Number 4.
> To bring him with us.

>   **LISA**
> What? To church? — He'll
> have to stay in the car.

Jennifer's smile drops.

INT. HALL OUTSIDE BEDROOMS - DAY

Lisa moves back to her bedroom, peaking inside.

INT. PARENT'S BEDROOM - DAY

Andrew is lying in bed, asleep. Lisa closes the door quietly.

EXT. FARMHOUSE AND ROAD - DAY

The Reeves' station wagon pulls out of the driveway and onto the road, driving off.

INT. CHURCH - DAY

Lisa, Clark, Jennifer, and Nicholas are sitting together, listening to the sermon. Jennifer turns her eyes to the church's doors.

EXT. CHURCH PARKING LOT - DAY

The Reeves' station wagon is parked amongst the other cars and trucks, all of which are slightly futuristic in design.

Number 4 is sitting in the back seat of the station wagon.

INT. STATION WAGON - DAY

Number 4 is staring at the church.

INT. CHURCH - DAY

Everybody kneels in unison. Lisa notices
that Nicholas is not wearing socks.
Black shoes, black pants, but no socks.
She whispers:

> **LISA**
> Nicholas, where are your
> socks?

> **NICHOLAS**
> Oops... I forgot.

EXT. TOWN'S MAIN STREET - DAY

The Reeves' station wagon drives into
the center of a small town. There are no
buildings higher than four stories and
everything - a movie theater, a hardware
store, a police station, a barber shop,
a grocery store, a bank, etc. - seems to
be located on its main street. The
Reeves' wagon pulls into the grocery
store parking lot.

INT. STATION WAGON - DAY

Lisa parks the car and gets out.

> **LISA**
> I'll just be a minute. I
> only have a couple of
> things to pick up.

Clark is seated in the passenger seat.
The two children are in the back with
Number 4.

EXT. TOWN'S MAIN STREET - DAY

Kevin is cruising down Main Street in
his fiery red convertible, looking for
trouble. Tim and Mark are with him. The
car's radio is turned up loud.

Kevin spots an attractive 16-year-old
GIRL walking on the sidewalk. He
whistles at her.

> **KEVIN**
> Hey sweet cheeks, want a
> ride?

The girl ignores them. Kevin slows,
driving alongside her.

KEVIN
Oh, come-on honey, I know
you want a ride. Don't
you?

Kevin laughs. Holding the clutch down,
he revs his engine loudly, eyeing the
girl. She enters a drug store to get
away from the boys. Kevin laughs.

KEVIN
Guess she didn't want a
ride after all.

Kevin peels out, stopping at a red light
up the street. He noticed the Reeves
station wagon in front of the nearby
grocery store. He sees Clark sitting
inside it.

KEVIN
Well, well, well, today
must be my luck day.

TIM
Mr. Bicycle.

KEVIN
In the flesh.

EXT. GROCERY STORE PARKING LOT - DAY

Clark is staring out the window at nothing in particular. Jennifer and Nicholas are talking to Number 4.

> **SHEILA** (O.S.)
> Clark?

SHEILA, an attractive 16 year old, is approaching the Reeves' wagon. She is carrying a bag of groceries.

> **CLARK**
> Oh, hi Sheila.

INT. STATION WAGON - DAY

Clark fumbles nervously with the door handle as he gets out of the car. He likes Sheila. Jennifer and Nicholas stare out at Sheila.

EXT. GROCERY STORE PARKING LOT - DAY

Clark steps over to Sheila, about ten feet away from the station wagon.

> **SHEILA**
> I thought that was you
> hiding in that car.

CLARK
Yeah, that was me. — It
is me.
(A beat)
Doing some shopping?

SHEILA
Oh, kind of. Just came
down to get my Mom some
milk and things. Anything
to drive the car. I got
my license on Saturday. I
still can't believe I
passed the test.

CLARK
That's great,
congratulations. It must—

Kevin's loud car rumbles up alongside
the station wagon, parking.

KEVIN
Hi Clark. Told ya I'd see
you around.

Kevin, Tim, and Mark get out of their
car. Sheila sees that the boys have
their fists clenched. She whispers:

SHEILA
Clark, I think you better

go into the store. — I'll
watch your little sister
and brother for you.

CLARK
No... I'll be alright.
(A beat)
You can go home, there's
nothing to worry about.
Go on.

INT. STATION WAGON - DAY

Jennifer and Nicholas watch the boys
pass their station wagon. Kevin glares
in at the children.

KEVIN
Don't touch me car.

Kevin leads Tim and Mark toward Clark.

NUMBER 4
Jennifer, what is happening? Who
are those boys?

JENNIFER
Bullies.

EXT. GROCERY STORE PARKING LOT - DAY

Clark moves several steps away from

Sheila as Kevin, Tim, and Mark arrive.

KEVIN
Talkin' to Sheila?

Kevin wiggles his bottom about.

KEVIN (CONTINUED)
— Miss cheer leader.
Maybe this bicycle boy is
straight after all.

SHEILA
Kevin — don't start
anything here. He's got
his little brother and
sister in the car.

KEVIN
Shut up Sheila.

Kevin moves up close to Clark.

KEVIN
So farm boy, how are
things out on that farm
of yours? It must be
really exciting. What you
been doing out there?
Countin' cows?

Tim and Mark laugh.

> **CLARK**
> No... Just watching the
> corn grow.

Sheila laughs.

> **KEVIN**
> Oh, you are such a wise
> ass.

Kevin punches Clark right in the nose,
knocking him to the pavement.

> **SHEILA**
> Kevin!

Kevin rushes Clark who is struggling to
rise. Clark, surprisingly, catches Kevin
with an uppercut to the chin. Kevin
staggers backwards and drops to one
knee.

INT. STATION WAGON - DAY

Jennifer and Nicholas squeal and clap
their hands.

EXT. GROCERY STORE PARKING LOT - DAY

Kevin growls out. Rushing Clark, he
grabs him in a bear hug.

KEVIN
Come-on! Hold him for me!

Tim and Mark rush in, grabbing Clark, twisting his arms behind his back. Kevin starts punching Clark, again and again.

SHEILA
Stop! — Kevin stop it!

She drops her grocery bag and grabs Kevin by the hair. He shoves her to the pavement, hard, immediately resuming his beating on Clark.

KEVIN
How do you like this wise ass! — Hugh? — Hugh?

Clark is taking a beating, soon he is no longer able to struggle against Tim and Mark.

INT. STATION WAGON - DAY

Nicholas starts crying. Jennifer turns to Number 4.

JENNIFER
— Number 4, you have to stop them. — They're hurting Clark. They're

hurting him bad. Number
4, do something. Please.
Do something! Help him.
Help him!

Number 4 is unsure what to do.

EXT. GROCERY STORE PARKING LOT - DAY

Tired, Kevin stops to catch his breath.
Blood is streaming from Clark's nose.

The back door of the Reeves station
wagon opens and Number 4 steps out.

> **TIM**
> Well, look at that, a
> robot dressed in farmer
> jeans.

> **KEVIN**
> So, Clarky boy's been
> dressing up robots. He
> likes to play dress up
> with big dolls.

They all chuckle.

Number 4 sees that blood dripping from
Clark's face. Opening his right,
skeleton-like hand, the robot swings it
away from his body, toward Kevin's

automobile. Pressing his metal
fingertips against the car, he then
starts walking toward the boys, deeply
scratching the length of the convertible
as he moves forward. The sound is
horrible.

Kevin can't believe it. Tim and Mark
drop Clark.

Kevin growls out and charges the robot.
Number 4 throws up his arms,
defensively, locking his elbows. Kevin
runs into the robots opened palms and is
sent to the pavement, hitting his head
upon the asphalt.

Number 4 turns to face Tim and Mark who
hesitate and then flee the scene.

Kevin sees his Tim and Mark running off
and then he loses consciousness.

Lisa and **OTHERS** come shuffling out of
the store. Jennifer and Nicholas runs
toward Clark.

                    LISA
          Clark!

EXT. GROECERY STORE PARKING LOT - DAY

A police car, lights flashing, is moving toward the gathering crowd.

FADE OUT

INT. LIVING ROOM - NIGHT

Clark is convalescing upon a reclined chair. He has a black eye and his face is bruised. Number 4 is sitting on the couch next to Clark, like a member of the family. The robot is now wearing a white, button up shirt with his farmer jeans. Jennifer and Nicholas are sitting besides the robot, flipping through a children's encyclopedia, looking at the pictures

Lisa and Andrew enter the room. Lisa places a bag of ice against Clark's black eye.

> **CLARK**
> More ice?

> **LISA**
> The doctor said to keep
> the swelling down and
> that means ice.

ANDREW
How do you feel?

CLARK
Kind of like I got run
over by a truck.

ANDREW
Kevin Brunner, that boy's
been nothing but trouble
since the day we moved
out here. — And those
other two, helping him
like that. I can't
understand it. I never
could stand bullies.

Lisa rubs Andrew's shoulders, calming
him.

CLARK
Well, thanks to Number 4,
I'm alive to disapprove
of bullies with you.

Lisa turns to Number 4, uncomfortable,
struggling to word things correctly.

LISA
Number 4, you should be,
I'd like to thank you
for, well, for doing
what you —

Flipping through the encyclopedia,
Nicholas accidentally tears a page in
half.

> ### ANDREW
> Nicholas, I thought I
> told you that you're not
> supposed to be looking
> through those
> encyclopedias without
> supervision.

> ### NICHOLAS
> But, I thought only
> Superman and Superdog
> have supervision?

The tension breaks and there is
laughter. Andrew scoops up Nicholas.

> ### ANDREW
> Okay, time for bed.

> ### JENNIFER
> I want a piggyback.

> ### ANDREW
> Well, climb on.

She leaps onto her father's back. Andrew
carries them toward their bedroom.

ANDREW
Off we go.

JENNIFER
Goodnight Number 4.

Number 4 does not want her to leave, it can be heard in his voice.

NUMBER 4
Goodnight Jennifer.

NICHOLAS
Goodnight Number 4.

NUMBER 4
Goodnight Nicholas.

And they're gone. Lisa turns back to Number 4.

LISA
Thanks again Number 4.
For helping Clark. For
helping us.

NUMBER 4
You are welcome Mrs. Reeves.

She heads out of the room.

> **LISA**
> (To Clark)
> You need anything, just
> call.

Clark notices the time. It is ten
o'clock.

> **CLARK**
> Can you turn on the TV?
> Channel 9.

> **LISA**
> Sure.

She does so before she leaves the room.
There is a commercial on.

> **CLARK**
> Number 4, I want you to
> watch this movie with me.
> I mean, if you want to.

Number 4 is confused.

> **NUMBER 4**
> I do not have to go out to the
> barn? To be turned off?

> **CLARK**
> No, not if you don't want
> to.

> **NUMBER 4**
> — I do not want to.

Clark smiles.

> **CLARK**
> So, you want to watch the movie?

> **NUMBER 4**
> I will watch the movie.

> **CLARK**
> Good. It's an old movie but I think you'll really like it. It has robots in it.

> **NUMBER 4**
> Robots?

Number 4 turns his full attention to the television. The commercial ends and the movie begins. After a 20th Century Fox introduction the words: "A LONG TIME AGO IN A GALAXY FAR, FAR AWAY..." appear on the television screen. The familiar music to Star Wars begins as the film's title appears.

INT. CHILDREN'S BEDROOM - NIGHT

Jennifer and Nicholas are both lying in bed awake. Lisa pops her head into the room.

>   **LISA**
> And how come you two are still awake?

>   **JENNIFER**
> Oh, we're just thinkin'.

Lisa enters the room, moving to Jennifer.

>   **LISA**
> About what?

>   **JENNIFER**
> About Number 4.

>   **LISA**
> What about Number 4?

>   **JENNIFER**
> Well, he's our friend and we don't ever want him to break or anything.

>   **NICHOLAS**
> Yeah, when Number 7

broke, Daddy took him
apart and put him on a
shelf.

LISA
Well, that's not
something that will ever
happen to Number 4. He's
a very special robot and
if he ever breaks down
your father will fix him
as good as new.

NICHOLAS
You promise?

LISA
I promise.

The children smile.

JENNIFER
Can you tell Number 4 to
come in to say goodnight
to us again? Please.

NICHOLAS
Please.

Lisa thinks for a moments.

                    LISA
All right. — But he's
watching a movie with
Clark right now so it
won't be until a
commercial, so until he
comes in I want you both
to get some sleep.

                 JENNIFER
We will.

                    LISA
You promise?

SIMULATENEOUS DIALOGUE

                 JENNIFER
I promise.

                 NICHOLAS
Promise.

END OF SIMULTANEOUS DIALOGUE

                    LISA
    Okay.

INT. LIVING ROOM - NIGHT

Clark and Number 4 are watching Star
Wars. Luke Skywalker is talking to the

robots C3PO and R2D2 and the scene has
Number 4's full attention.

INT. CHILDREN'S BEDROOM - NIGHT

Number 4 enters, his lighted brain
brightening the darkness. He sits down
besides Jennifer as she slowly awakens.

> **JENNIFER**
> ... Number 4...

Number 4 keeps his voice low.

> **NUMBER 4**
> Hello Jennifer, your mother
> instructed me to visit you.

> **JENNIFER**
> I know, I was waiting for
> you.
> (A beat)
> I just wanted to say
> goodnight to you again...
> and tell you that you're
> a great robot.

Number 4 is touched.

> **NUMBER 4**
> Thank you.

>   **JENNIFER**
> I'm sorry that I ever
> called you names...
> You're eyes aren't empty.
> They're full.

Again, Number 4's voice is full of
emotion.

>   **NUMBER 4**
> Thank you...

>   **JENNIFER**
> Can you tell me a bedtime
> story?

>   **NUMBER 4**
> But, I do not know any bedtime
> stories.

>   **JENNIFER**
> Please.

He cannot say no to her.

>   **NUMBER 4**
> Okay.

Number 4 thinks for a moment and then:

>   **NUMBER 4**
> A long time ago in a galaxy far,
> far away...

EXT. FARMHOUSE - NIGHT

The moon's glow paints the farmhouse
with it dim light. Crickets chirp.

EXT. TOWN'S MAIN STREET - NIGHT

The town's police station is located on
Main Street. Kevin's red convertible is
parked outside, alongside a police car.
A dark sedan pulls into the parking lot.

INT. CELL AND HALL - NIGHT

Kevin is lying on a small bed located
beneath a barred window, which is
casting its shadows across his angry
face. Awake, he is staring at the
ceiling.

A door clicks open at the end of the
outside hall and a **TALL POLICEMAN** moves
to Kevin. He unlocks the boy's cell door
with a credit card shaped, plastic key.

>   **TALL POLICEMAN**
>   Okay Kevin, time to go.
>   Your father's here.

INT. POLICE STATION - NIGHT

Kevin's father, **MR. BRUNNER**, is standing before a **BALDING OFFICER**. Brunner is a large, unfriendly man dressed in a dark suit. He is angry.

                    MR. BRUNNER
          I still can't believe
          that you went and locked
          him up. He's in high
          school for Christ's
          sakes. Didn't you ever
          have a fist fight when
          you were in school? — I
          mean, he's a kid and when
          you're a kid you get into
          fights. It's just the way
          things are.

                    BALDING OFFICER
          Mr. Brunner, we don't
          have a juvenile detention
          center in this town. We
          had to wait for you to
          pick him up. The other
          two boys were picked up
          by their parents early
          this afternoon.

                    MR. BRUNNER
Yeah, well, I was out of
town.

                    BALDING OFFICER
That's why we had to keep
him here.

The door behind the officer opens and
the tall policeman escorts Kevin
forward.

                    MR. BRUNNER
You all right boy?

Kevin nods yes.

                    MR. BRUNNER
Then let's get out of
here.

Brunner grabs his son by the arm and
starts out but is stopped by the balding
officer.

                    BALDING OFFICER
— Now wait just one
minute. Before you two
waltz out of here I want
you both to know that the
only reason that this is
all being swept under the

carpet is because the
Reeves decided not to
press charges. If they
did, your son would have
been turned over to the
Juvenile Court in
Appleton.

Brunner burns a stare in to the balding
officer.

> **MR. BRUNNER**
> Are you through?

> **BALDING OFFICER**
> Yes.

> **MR. BRUNNER**
> Then get out of my way.

The officer slowly steps aside.

EXT. POLICE STATION - NIGHT

Brunner pulls Kevin away from the
station, spinning the boy about.

> **MR. BRUNNER**
> Kevin, I've just about
> had it with you. If you
> ever embarrass me like
> this again you'll wish

you were never born.

Kevin is staring at the pavement.
Brunner slaps him across the face, hard.

                    MR. BRUNNER
You listening to me?

Kevin pulls away from his father and
heads for his convertible.

                    MR. BRUNNER
          — And where the hell do
          you think you're going?

Kevin answers without looking back.

                    KEVIN
          Have to drive my car
          home.

Brunner stomps off in the opposite
direction, heading for his dark sedan.

Kevin stops before his car, angrily
staring at the scratches along its side.

EXT. FARM - DAY

A slightly futuristic truck, towing a
small cart, is bumping down a dirt road
that leads away from the farmhouse and

to its back fields. Andrew is driving the truck. Robots 1, 2, 3, and 4 are sitting behind him.

The truck enters the fields behind the farmhouse.

EXT. FIELDS - DAY

The truck bumps down the road, which runs between two planted fields. Number 4 is looking about, examining his surroundings.

The truck disappears down the road.

EXT. FIELD BY ROAD - DAY

The truck rumbles forward, parking alongside a large cornfield. The Reeves farmhouse is no longer in sight.

On the other side of the cornfield, approximately 100 yards distant, a pick up truck passes by, driving down a double lane road that disappears into the distance.

> **ANDREW**
> Number 4, this is the field.

Andrew pulls a lever, releasing the cart
behind the truck. It rolls backward
several feet and then stops.

> **ANDREW** (CONTINUED)
> I'll be back before dark
> to pick you up. Will you
> be all right?

Number 4 exists the truck.

> **NUMBER 4**
> Yes, I believe so.

> **ANDREW**
> Good. Number 1, Number 2,
> Number 3, you'll work
> here under Number 4's
> supervision.

The robots climb out of the truck.

> **ANDREW**
> Remember, 30 feet apart.

> **NUMBER 4**
> 30 feet apart.

As the truck drives off, the robots line
up in numerical order before Number 4.
Number 4 stands motionless watching
Andrew's truck until it disappears from

sight. Apprehensively, he then turns to
the robots. They are silent and
motionless.

> **NUMBER 4**
> Number 1, Number 2, Number 3...
> (A beat)
> Mr. Reeves will return for us
> sometime before sunset. We will
> work on installing the repellers until
> that time.

Silent, the three robots stare at Number
4. After a moment:

> **NUMBER 4**
> Go to work.

The robots move to the detached cart. It
is neatly packed with several large
mallets, dozens of basketball size
metallic spheres, and an equal number of
long silver poles that are pointed on
one end, like stakes.

EXT. TIM'S HOUSE - DAY

Kevin, in his convertible, pulls up to a
house located near town. Mark is sitting
in the back seat. Kevin leans on the
horn, which blares.

Tim comes out of the house, climbing into the car. The car speeds off.

INT. KEVIN'S CAR - DAY

Tim sees an aluminum baseball bat on the front seat.

> TIM
> What's with the bat?
> (Joking)
> What're we going to do,
> play baseball?

Mark laughs, Kevin doesn't. Kevin turns left at a fork in the road.

> TIM
> Where're we going?

Kevin doesn't answer. Tim turns to Mark.

> TIM
> Clark's?

Mark nods yes. Tim mumbles:

> TIM
> Oh, shit.

EXT. ROAD - DAY

Kevin's car speeds down the road.

EXT. FIELD BY ROAD - DAY

Four of the cart's metal poles have been driven into the earth, positioned between the trail and the cornfield. They are standing five feet above the ground. Arranged in a line, the poles are spaced 30 feet apart and metallic spheres have been secured atop the first three poles.

Number 4 is attaching a sphere to the four pole in line. Thirty feet distant, Reeve's other robots are using large mallets to drive a fifth pole into the ground.

Number 4 completes the task and steps back to examine his work. He notices something on the ground and picks it up. It is a bird's feather. It is bight blue. Holding it before his large eyes, he twists it about in the sunlight, enjoying its beauty.

EXT. ROAD BY FIELD - DAY

Kevin's car flashes by, traveling down

the road behind the Reeve's back
cornfields.

INT. KEVIN'S CAR - DAY

Out of the corner of his eye, Kevin
notices Reeves' robots working on the
far side of the cornfield they are
passing. He recognizes Number 4, who is
wearing clothing.

Kevin slams on the breaks.

EXT. ROAD BY FIELD - DAY

Kevin's convertible skids down the road.

EXT. FIELD BY ROAD - DAY

Number 4 hears the skidding car and
looks toward the road.

EXT. ROAD BY FIELD - DAY

The car stops.

> **TIM**
> — What are you trying to
> do, kill us?

Kevin shuts off the car and grabs his
bat.

                KEVIN
There. — The one with the
clothes. That's the one
from yesterday.

                MARK
They're alone. Nobody's
around.

Kevin heads for the cornfield.

                KEVIN
Come-on.

Mark follows Kevin. Tim hesitates and
then does the same.

EXT. FIELD BY ROAD - DAY

Robots 1, 2, and 3 continue to work,
paying no attention to the approaching
teenagers. Number 4 is not sure what to
make of them.

Kevin plows his way through the field,
bending over stalks of corn.

Number 4 recognizes Kevin and becomes
nervous.

Kevin pushes out of the tall corn stalks
and steps up to Number 4.

NUMBER 4
... What do you want?

KEVIN
You.

Kevin smashes the bat against the left side of Number 4's head. A bright light sparks within his dented brain cap. Dropping his feather, Number 4 falls to his knees, shocked, disorientated.

KEVIN
Nobody messes with me or my car. — Especially one of Clarky's tin dolls!

Kevin smashes the bat down upon Number 4's head, sending a crack spider webbing across the robot's brain cap. Kevin swings the bat again, smacking it against Number 4's right hip. Number 4 falls to the ground, landing on his side.

Kevin starts to batter Number 4, denting the robot's body.

Mark and Tim step out of the cornfield. They notice that the other robots have stopped working and are moving toward Kevin.

                    TIM
          Kevin...

Kevin ignores the call, continuing to
batter Number 4 who has rolled onto his
stomach and is attempting to crawl away.

                    TIM
          Kevin!

Kevin turns to Tim who points out the
approaching robots. They are carrying
large mallets. Kevin readies his bat.

                    TIM
          Kevin?

                    KEVIN
          You two take off on me
          this time and I'll kill
          you.

Dazed, Number 4 looks up to see the
approaching robots.

                  NUMBER 1
              (Emotionless)
          Number 4, these men are
          damaging you. What do you
          want us to do?

KEVIN
Aw, they ain't shit.

Kevin smashes Number 1 in the head, knocking the robot to its knees.

Number 2 and Number 3 stop. They do not know what to do. Kevin laughs and strikes them both down with his bat.

Kevin tosses his bat backward and pulls the large mallet from Number 1's skeleton-like hand. Bouncing, the bat lands besides Number 4.

KEVIN
Grab their hammers.

Kevin swings the mallet down on Number 1, shattering the robot's brain cap into a million pieces.

Tim and Mark go for the other hammers.

Number 4, filled with horror, struggles to rise.

NUMBER 4
No! — Stop! Stop!

Kevin swings the mallet down on Number 1 again, smashing its unprotected brain.

The lights in the brain go out and the
robot collapses, dead.

NUMBER 4
... No...

KEVIN
Well, well, the one with
the clothes hasn't had
enough.
(To Tim and Mark)
— Finish off those other
two while I personally
smash Clark's tin doll
into scrap metal.

Kevin approaches Number 4. Number 4 does
not know what to do. He looks for help
but there is none.

Tim and Mark smash the hammers down on
robots 2 and 3.

NUMBER 4
No. — Stop. Please stop.

Number 4 rises to his knees. Kevin bangs
the mallet down on Number 4's right
shoulder, denting him badly.

There is a harsh sound of glass
shattering. Number 4 sees Number 2

collapsing, dead.

Kevin lifts his hammer high.

KEVIN
You're next!

Number 4 notices the bat lying besides him. Kevin starts to swing his hammer down. Number 4, in desperation, grabs the bat, and swings it with blinding speed.

Tim and Mark hear a loud thud sound. They turn toward Number 4. Shocked and frightened they drop their hammers and flee, running into the cornfield, heading for the car.

Slowly, Number 4 rises to his feet, standing over Kevin's body. Kevin's head is twisted completely around.

Number 4 drops the bat, standing motionless. He looks at the robots lying lifeless on the ground, then to the fleeing boys, and then, down at dead Kevin Brunner.

NUMBER 4
No... no...

A moment passes.

EXT. BARNYARD - DAY

Jennifer and Nicholas are skipping
across the barnyard, heading toward the
small barn that houses the robots.

INT. SMALL BARN - DAY

The children enter the barn. Andrew and
Clark are within, working on the
Japanese robot.

> **JENNIFER**
> Hi Dad, hi Clark.

SIMULTANEOUS DIALOGUE

> **ANDREW**
> Hi honey.

> **CLARK**
> Hey Jennifer, what's up?

END OF SIMULTANEOUS DIALOGUE

Jennifer notices robots 5 and 6, seated
lifelessly on the bench.

> **JENNIFER**
> Dad, where's Number 4?

NICHOLAS
Yeah, we want to play
with him.

Andrew replies without turning away from
his work.

ANDREW
I have him out in the
back cornfield with 1, 2
and 3... They're putting
up a special type of
fence for me.

JENNIFER
What type of fence Dad?

ANDREW
Well, it's a fence that's
supposed to keep out
insects, repelling them
with a special, high
pitched sound.

CLARK
You really think it'll
work Dad?

ANDREW
I don't know. I guess
we'll find out next year
when we don't spray that
back field.

> JENNIFER
>
> Dad, can we go out to the
> back field to watch
> Number 4?

> ANDREW
>
> Yeah, sure, but tell your
> mother where you'll be,
> okay?

> JENNIFER
>
> Okay.

The children run out of the barn.

EXT. BARNYARD - DAY

The children run toward Lisa who is
placing new straw in the dog pen.
Cleopatra barks, waging her tail.

> JENNIFER
>
> Mom...

Lisa turns to them and slowly her face
goes pale. The children turn to see what
their mother is looking at and their
smiles disappear.

> LISA
>
> Andrew...

INT. SMALL BARN - DAY

Andrew and Clark are still working on the Japanese robot.

> **LISA** (O.S.)
> Andrew!

She sounds frightened.

> **LISA** (O.S. CONTINUED)
> ANDREW!

Andrew and Clark rush out of the barn.

EXT. BARNYARD - DAY

Andrew and Clark slow as they join Lisa and the children in the center of the yard.

Number 4 is limping toward them, carrying Kevin's limp, dead, body. Number 4 is confused, frightened, and in turmoil.

> **CLARK**
> ... Kevin Brunner...

> **ANDREW**
> Number 4... What happened?

Number 4 looks down at Jennifer and
Nicholas who are staring at him,
shocked, afraid.

> **ANDREW**
> Number 4?

> **NUMBER 4**
> Mr. Reeves... Clark... I did not
> know what to do. I did not mean
> to kill him.

> **ANDREW**
> Kill him? You killed him?
> Why?

Again, Number 4 looks to Jennifer and
Nicholas. Frightened, the children pull
close to their mother.

> **ANDREW**
> Number 4, put the boy
> down, and tell me what
> happened. Now.

Number 4 is very frightened. He
hesitates and then gently lies Kevin's
body down.

> **NUMBER 4**
> I, I did not mean to kill him.
> (A beat)

I tried to get away but I could not.
Then, the bullies, they killed
Number 1 and Number 3... They
were going to kill me.

CLARK
It was self-defense. Dad,
it was self-defense.

ANDREW
Number 4... Did you kill
Kevin Brunner to prevent
him from destroying you?

NUMBER 4
Yes. I was afraid, I did not want to
die. My continued existence is
important...
(Realizing it)
I am important. My...
(Looks at Jennifer)
My eyes are full.

ANDREW
... I understand.
(A beat)
The other "bullies,"
Kevin's friends, did
you... Were they hurt?

NUMBER 4
— No.

> **ANDREW**
> Where are they?

> **NUMBER 4**
> I do not know. They ran away.

> **ANDREW**
> But they helped Kevin
> destroy the other robots?

> **NUMBER 4**
> Yes... I asked them to stop... but
> they would not.

A loud police siren spins them all
about. A streamlined police car turns
off the road before the farmhouse and
rolls toward them. Its siren shuts off
but its flashing lights remain on. The
German Shepherd starts barking from her
pen.

> **LISA**
> Andrew?

> **JENNIFER**
> They're coming to take
> Number 4 away, aren't
> they?

The tall policeman who had let Kevin out
of his cell is the first out of the

police car, followed by the **LEAN POLICEMAN**. Both men are serious, alert, and ready for action. The tall officer is speaking into a hand microphone.

> **TALL POLICEMAN**
> We've found the boy's
> body and the robot.
> Repeat, we've found the
> boy's body and the robot.

The lean police officer draws out his gun, aiming the weapon at Number 4. Number 4 backs up a step.

> **LEAN POLICEMAN**
> Reeves, we're here for
> the robot.How do you turn
> it off?

> **NUMBER 4**
> Turn me off?

> **CLARK**
> But it was an accident.
> Self-defense. Kevin was
> tr —

> **LEAN POLICEMAN**
> — How do you turn it off!

Nicholas starts to cry.

JENNIFER
No! — You can't take him.
He's our friend. You
can't take him. He's
ours!

The officer aims his weapon at Number
4's lighted brain.

ANDREW
— I'll do it. I'll turn
him off.

Andrew steps between the officer and
Number 4, who steps back, nervous.

NUMBER 4
No... You will not turn me back on.

ANDREW
No, no. Everything's
going to be all right.

Number 4 looks at the policemen.

NUMBER 4
I do not want to be turned off. I
do not want them to take me
away from here.

ANDREW
Number 4, please... I

don't want any harm to
come to you. Now, if I
don't turn you off, these
men might damage you
severely trying to do so.

Number 4 is not swayed.

> **ANDREW**
> You won't be alone. I'll
> go with you and the
> policemen.
> (A beat)
> You're going to have to
> trust me.

A long moment and then:

> **NUMBER 4**
> ... I will trust you.

Andrew places his finger on Number 4's
chest button. Number 4 looks into
Andrew's eyes. Andrew pushed the button.
The lights disappear from Number 4's
brain and he falls forward, into
Andrew's arms.

Jennifer's eyes swell with tears.

FADE OUT

Niko Zinovii

Act Three

Niko Zinovii

FADE IN:

INT. HALL AND CELL - DAY

The two policemen drag Number 4's deactivated body to the cell that Kevin was in last night.

One of the cops opens the door with a special plastic key-card and they toss Number 4 inside. He hits the stone floor hard, landing in the shadows.

INT. POLICE STATION - DAY

Andrew is pacing, thinking. The balding police officer enters the room. He tries to ease the tension.

> **BALDING OFFICER**
> Hello Mr. Reeves. How's Clark?

> **ANDREW**
> Oh, he's slowly healing up. Those boys beat him up pretty badly.

> **BALDING OFFICER**
> Yeah, I know. It's too bad that had to happen.
> (A beat)

Let's sit down.

They do so.

> **BALDING OFFICER**
> Mr. Reeves, Tim Berrell
> and Mark Leverk have both
> admitted to intentionally
> destroying three of your
> robots. Your property.
> They're temporarily
> under home arrest. Kevin
> Brunner, who led these
> boys in damaging your
> property is dead. Killed
> by one of your robots.
> (A beat)
> Now, I don't really know
> much about robots, but I
> do know one thing.
> They're machines. And as
> machines, they only do
> what they're told to do.

He looks at Andrew long and hard.

> **ANDREW**
> What, are you saying that
> Number 4 was instructed
> to kill Kevin Brunner?

BALDING OFFICER

Look, I know that you and
your family were upset
over what happened to
Clark. Did anybody...
You, your wife, your
children, did any of you
say something out of
anger that the robot
might have misinterpreted
as an order? Like, "That
Kevin, I wish he was
dead."

ANDREW

No, nothing like that.

BALDING OFFICER

Are you sure?

ANDREW

Yes, I'm positive. Nobody
programmed Number 4 to
kill that boy,
accidentally or
intentionally. That's not
what happened.

BALDING OFFICER

Well, then what did
happen? The boys'
testimony makes it clear

that the robot
deliberately struck and
killed Kevin Brunner. Not
by accident. It was a
deliberate act. And for a
robot to carry out such
an act, it would have to
be directed to do so.

ANDREW
Not if... Not if the
robot can think.

BALDING OFFICER
Excuse me?

ANDREW
It was self-defense.
Those boys were trying to
"kill" Number 4 and he
defended himself.

BALDING OFFICER
Defended himself? What
are you talking about?
This is a robot, a
machine.

Andrew is silent for a moment.

ANDREW
Number 4... He's not just

a machine. He's the first
robot in our history to
possess sentient
artificial intelligence.
He's alive, he has a mind
of his own. A short time
ago my son modified a
government micro-cortex
and implanted it into the
robot's brain. Number 4
can now think, just you
or I. And just like us,
he can carry out
deliberate acts
independent of
instructions.
          (A beat)
He killed Kevin Brunner,
yes, but it was in self-
defense. It was
unintentional. He was
only protecting himself.

The officer sits back in his seat,
taking it all in. After several long
moments:

                    BALDING OFFICER
          Once we record your
          robot's memory, as long
          as the robot wasn't
          instructed to perform the

act, the new robot laws
will free you from any
possible charges of
negligence or wrongful
death. You do understand
that, don't you?

Andrew nods yes.

>   **BALDING OFFICER**
> Then why all this about
> self-defense?

>   **ANDREW**
> Because it's the truth.

>   **BALDING OFFICER**
> A robot killing a person
> in self-defense. People
> will never accept
> something like that.
> It'll only stir up a lot
> of unnecessary trouble. A
> whole lot of trouble.

>   **ANDREW**
> I'm sorry, but, like I
> said, it's the truth.

The officer is silent for a long moment
and then:

> **BALDING OFFICER**
> Wait a minute, this thing
> that you say your son put
> into the robot's brain.
> You said that it was
> government. Where did it
> come from?

EXT. FARMHOUSE ROOF - NIGHT

The night sky is clouded, alit by a
waning moon, and speckled by dim stars.

The weather vane on the roof is
motionless, blanketed by shadows.

EXT. BARNYARD - NIGHT

An **OWL**, perched in a tree, hoots.

INT. PARENT'S BEDROOM - NIGHT

Lisa, wearing a nightgown, is sitting on
the bed. Andrew is undressing.

> **LISA**
> So, there's nothing that
> we can do?

> **ANDREW**
> No. As soon as I told him
> where the micro-cortex

came from he made up his
mind. Passing the
'problem' up. He has some
men from the government
coming out tomorrow to
pick up Number 4 and take
him away. I told Clark
but I don't think we
should say anything to
Jennifer and Nicholas.
Not until after.

EXT. HALL OUTSIDE BEDROOMS - NIGHT

Jennifer and Nicholas, in pajamas, are
eaves dropping on their parent's
conversation.

> **LISA** (O.S.)
> But... How can they just
> take him away? I mean, we
> do own him.

> **ANDREW** (O.S.)
> But we don't own the
> micro-cortex. It works
> and the government wants
> it back, so they're going
> to take his brain apart
> to get it. Then, when
> they have it, they'll
> ship Number 4 back to us,

probably in pieces, and
he won't be the same.
What made him unique will
be missing. He'll just be
an empty headed robot.
He'll be dead.

Jennifer can't bear it. She pulls
Nicholas into their bedroom.

INT. CHILDREN'S BEDROOM - NIGHT

Jennifer closes their bedroom door. She
wipes a tear from her brother's cheek.

> **JENNIFER**
> Don't cry Nicholas...

> **NICHOLAS**
> But Daddy said that the
> men are going to take
> Number 4 apart. Make him
> dead. Tomorrow.

> **JENNIFER**
> I know.
> (A beat)
> Well... I guess then it's
> up to us to help him.

> **NICHOLAS**
> Help him?

                    JENNIFER
          Yeah, help him. He's our
          friend and you always
          help your friends when
          they're in trouble. — And
          nobody is going to make
          him empty again... It
          just wouldn't be right.

                    NICHOLAS
          Yeah.

INT. PARENT'S BEDROOM - NIGHT

Lisa is lying in bed, staring at the
ceiling. Andrew slides in alongside her.
After a moment of silence:

                    ANDREW
          What bothers me the most
          is that I asked him to
          trust me.

He turns off the lamp and the room goes
dark.

INT. CLARK'S BEDROOM - NIGHT

The room is dark. Clark is lying in bed,
staring up at the ceiling.

INT. CHILDREN'S BEDROOM - NIGHT

The beds are empty.

EXT. FARMHOUSE - NIGHT

Jennifer and Nicholas, dressed, are
sneaking out the back door. They move to
Clark's bicycle.

EXT. ROAD IN FRONT OF FARMHOUSE - NIGHT

The children push the bicycle up onto
the road and awkwardly mount it. The
bike is large for them and it is
difficult. Nicholas drops down on the
seat and holds on as Jennifer pedals
away, standing, straining.

Swaying from side to side, the bicycle
becomes smaller and smaller as it
travels away from the farmstead.
Finally, it disappears into the
darkness.

INT. BARRROOM - NIGHT

A cue ball breaks up a rack, scattering
the balls about the pool table.

The smoke filled bar is small. A couple
of **MEN** and **WOMEN** are playing pool. Three

CUSTOMERS are seated at the bar, drinking quietly.

Mr. Brunner, angry, enters, moving to the bar.

> **BARTENDER**
> I heard about Kevin. You must be mad as hell.

> **MR. BRUNNER**
> Just give me a beer.

> **BARTENDER**
> Sure thing.

EXT. BAR - NIGHT

The tiny bar is at the end of the town's main street.

EXT. POLICE STATION - NIGHT

All is quiet. A traffic light changes from red to green. A lone car drives by.

INT. CELL - NIGHT

Number 4 is still lying on the cell's floor, deactivated.

EXT. TOWN'S MAIN STREET - NIGHT

Jennifer and Nicholas pedal up the
street on the bicycle, dismounting
across the street from the police
station. They look about. No one is
around. They whisper:

> **NICHOLAS**
> What do we do now?

> **JENNIFER**
> Come-on, follow me.

She sneaks toward the police station.

EXT. POLICE STATION - NIGHT

Crossing the street, the children hide
in the shadows of the building.

Jennifer spies a lighted window. She
steps up on a plastic crate and peeks
inside.

INT. POLICE STATION - NIGHT

Jennifer's face appears in the window
located behind the balding officer who
is sitting at a desk, doing paperwork.
Tired, he yawns and turns on a radio
that plays country music.

Jennifer looks about the room.

EXT. POLICE STATION - NIGHT

Jennifer steps down from the window, whispering.

> **JENNIFER**
> He's not in there.

Jennifer leads Nicholas along the side of the building.

> **JENNIFER**
> He must be somewhere
> else. They must be
> keeping him -

She notices a small barred window at ground level. She kneels, peering inside.

INT. CELL - NIGHT

Jennifer is looking into Number 4's cell. She sees the robot lying on the floor. Nicholas joins her. They whisper:

> **NICHOLAS**
> Number 4 — Number 4.

Number 4 does not respond.

> **JENNIFER**
> Shhh! He's turned off, he
> can't hear you.

> **NICHOLAS**
> How can we get him out of
> there?

> **JENNIFER**
> I don't know, but there
> has to be a way.

EXT. POLICE STATION - NIGHT

Jennifer sits down, thinking.

Nicholas leans forward, sticking his
head between the window's bars.

> **JENNIFER**
> — Nicholas! You can fit
> through the bars.

> **NICHOLAS**
> Yeah.

Nicholas squeezes between the bars.

INT. CELL - NIGHT

Jennifer lowers Nicholas down into the
cell. Nicholas drops upon the room's
bed.

> **JENNIFER**
> You okay?

> **NICHOLAS**
> Yeah.

> **JENNIFER**
> Then turn him on.

Nicholas moves over to Number 4.

> **JENNIFER**
> Go on, turn him on.

Nicholas does so. Number 4's brain
lights up and he sits upright.

> **NUMBER 4**
> Nicholas? What happened?
> Where am I?

> **JENNIFER**
> Number 4.

He turns to her.

> **NUMBER 4**
> Jennifer? Jennifer, where am I?

> **JENNIFER**
> Shhh! You're in jail and
> me and Nicholas came to

rescue you. Come mornin'
the police are going to
give you to some people
who are going to take
your brain apart. But me
and Nicholas aren't going
to let that happen. We're
going to get you out of
here and hide you back at
the farm.

NUMBER 4
Hide me? Back at the farm?

JENNIFER
If we don't they'll take
you apart. You'll be
dead.

NUMBER 4
I will hide. But... How can I leave
this place?

Jennifer grabs onto the window's bars,
pulling on them.

JENNIFER
Well, I've been thinkin'.
Your muscles, they're
made out of steel. I bet
you're strong enough to
pull out these bars. And
then you can climb out.

NUMBER 4
Pull out the bars?

JENNIFER
Yeah, try to pull them
out. I just know you can
do it.

NUMBER 4
I will try.

Number 4 limps to the window, climbing
atop the bed.

JENNIFER
Now grab onto one of
these bars and pull.

Number 4 does so apprehensively,
wrapping his skeleton-like fingers
around the bar.

JENNIFER
That's it, now pull.

Number 4 starts to pull. The lights
within his brain surge, becoming
brighter as he does so. The bar does not
move.

JENNIFER
Pull harder Number 4.
Pull harder.

Number 4 increases his effort, his brain glowing even brighter. The bar starts to bend and the cement cracks.

> **JENNIFER**
> That's it. — Keep pulling.

Number 4 jerks backward as the bar tears loose, sending crumbling cement sprinkling across the cell. The light from his brain dims with the cessation of effort, returning to its normal brightness.

INT. POLICE STATION - NIGHT

The balding officer continues with his paperwork, listening to country music. (He has not heard what is happening in the cell.)

INT. CELL - NIGHT

> **JENNIFER**
> I knew you could do it.
> Now pull out another one.

Number 4 grabs another bar. As he pulls his brain brightens.

INT. POLICE STATION - NIGHT

The officer pours himself a cup of
coffee and slowly returns to his desk.

EXT. POLICE STATION - NIGHT

Jennifer and Nicholas are pulling Number
4 up out of the window. Once out, Number
4 staggers, leaning against the
building. The light in his brain dims
and then returns to normal.

> **NUMBER 4**
> My battery is low. I am running out
> of power. I do not know if I can
> travel.

> **JENNIFER**
> But... But Number 4, you
> have to make it back to
> the farm with us. If you
> don't, they'll catch you
> and kill you. Please try.
> I don't want to lose you.
> You're the very best
> friend I ever had.

Number 4 looks into her eyes. Summing up
his strength, he pushes himself off the
wall.

EXT. TOWN'S MAIN STREET - NIGHT

Limping and moving slowly, Number 4
follows the children to the bicycle
located across the street.

INT. BARROOM - NIGHT

Mr. Brunner, intoxicated, is drinking at
the bar. Brunner, the bartender and
three other men are the only people
remaining in the bar. (The **BLONDE MAN**,
the **BEARDED MAN**, and the **SKINNY MAN**.)

> **BARTENDER**
> So, this Reeves arranged
> with the police to give
> this robot of his to the
> government and nobody's
> getting arrested?

> **MR. BRUNNER**
> That's right.

> **SKINNY MAN**
> I can't believe this. I
> mean, that thing went and
> killed your son. Your
> son's dead and the police
> aren't doing nothin'
> about it.

MR. BRUNNER
Nope.

BLONDE MAN
But, why aren't they
arresting this Reeves
guy? After all, he owns
the damn thing, doesn't
he?

MR. BRUNNER
They say Reeves isn't
responsible. That this
robot wasn't told to kill
my Kevin. That Reeves is
off the hook because this
thing can actually think
by itself.

BARTENDER
Think by itself?

MR. BRUNNER
That's what they say.
That's why they're
turning the thing over to
the feds.

BEARDED MAN
Well, I say that's a load
of bull.

BLONDE MAN

You got that right. I say
he is responsible.

MR. BRUNNER

No, it was that damn
robot that killed my
Kevin. — I'm holding that
murdering thing
responsible. According to
the police, it knew
exactly what it was
doing. I want it
destroyed. Not turned
over to the government.
Destroyed.

BARTENDER

Where is this robot?
Probably still with
Reeves, don't you think?

MR. BRUNNER

I don't know.

BEARDED MAN

Well, I say why don't we
go on out to this Reeves'
farm tonight and pay him
a little visit. Let him
know how we all feel
about this. Tell him that

we want his robot. —Or
else. What do you say?

> ### MR. BRUNNER
> I say that sounds like an
> excellent idea.

EXT. ROAD BY FIELD - NIGHT

Number 4 is sitting on the bicycle seat,
holding Nicholas. Standing, Jennifer is
pedaling the bike as before. She is
struggling, tired. The light emanating
from Number 4's brain has grown dimmer.

> ### JENNIFER
> See Number 4, you're
> going to make it. We're
> almost back home, just a
> little farther.

> ### NUMBER 4
> (Weak)
> ... Just a little further...

EXT. ROAD - NIGHT

A futuristic but beat up pickup truck
speeds down the road.

INT. PICKUP TRUCK - NIGHT

Brunner, the bartender, and the three men from the bar are seated within. The skinny man is driving. Brunner is besides him.

> **SKINNY MAN**
> Hey, what's that up there?

> **BARTENDER**
> I don't know, looks like a couple of kids on a bike.

EXT. ROAD BY FIELD - NIGHT

Jennifer notices the approaching headlights and then the truck zooms by them, almost knocking them over.

> **JENNIFER**
> Boy, they're drivin' fast. I won —

The truck skids to a stop a hundred yards down the road.

Down the road: Brunner sticks his head out the window, looking back.

> ### MR. BRUNNER
> Those are two of the
> Reeves' kids! And they
> have that robot with
> them. The one with the
> clothes. — The one that
> killed my boy!

INT. PICKUP TRUCK - NIGHT

Brunner pulls back inside.

> ### MR. BRUNNER
> — Turn around. Let's get
> that robot!

EXT. ROAD BY FIELD - NIGHT

The truck turns about and roars toward
the children and Number 4.

INT. PICKUP TRUCK - NIGHT

The truck is speeding toward the
bicycle.

Brunner grabs the steering wheel,
turning the truck, pointing it directly
at the children and Number 4.

EXT. ROAD BY FIELD - NIGHT

The truck is coming right at the
children and Number 4.

NUMBER 4
Jennifer, what is happening?

INT. PICKUP TRUCK - NIGHT

The truck's driver fights with Brunner
for control.

SKINNY MAN
— Hey, let go! What are
you tryin' —

Brunner swings over a foot, pressing
down on the gas pedal.

EXT. ROAD BY FIELD - NIGHT

The truck is coming straight at the
bicycle, about to hit the children and
Number 4. Jennifer turns off the road.

EXT. FIELD BY ROAD - NIGHT

The bike rumbles down into the Reeve's
back cornfield, zipping through the high
stalks of corn.

EXT. ROAD BY FIELD - NIGHT

The pickup truck skids to a stop.

INT. PICKUP TRUCK - NIGHT

Brunner looks back into the field. He can see Number 4's lighted brain cap rapidly moving through the stalks of corn.

> **SKINNY MAN**
> Hey! — What are you trying to do? You could have killed those kids!

Brunner scrambles out of the truck.

EXT. ROAD BY FIELD - NIGHT

> **SKINNY MAN**
> Hey, where're you goin'?

> **MR. BRUNNER**
> After that robot. And when I get it I'm going to smash it into a million pieces. — You three coming with me or not?

The men look at one another indecisively.

MR. BRUNNER
Damn it, that thing
killed my son. Are you
going to just sit there
on your asses or help me
deal out some justice?

The bearded man gets out of the truck.

BEARDED MAN
I'm in.

SKINNY MAN
Okay, okay, but no
hurting the kids.

MR. BRUNNER
Wouldn't dream of it.

EXT. FIELD BY ROAD - NIGHT

The bicycle emerges from the cornfield.
Jennifer loses control and they all fall
to the ground. Jennifer sees that
Brunner and his men are moving down into
the field.

JENNIFER
Oh no... They must be
after Number 4.

Nicholas is trying, unsuccessfully, to
help Number 4 to his feet. Low on power
he cannot rise. Jennifer helps.

> **JENNIFER**
> Number 4... You gotta get
> up. Come-on. Those men
> are comin' to get you.
> You gotta get up!

They manage to pull Number 4 to his
feet.

> **NUMBER 4**
> I am sorry Jennifer but... I am
> almost out of power...

> **JENNIFER**
> I don't care. — You're
> gonna make it back to the
> house. Now, come-on!

She grabs Number 4, yanking him down the
dirt path that leads to their home.

In the field: Brunner whacks the stalks
of corn out of his way. The three men
are right behind him. Brunner sees that
light emanating from Number 4's brain
disappear into the darkness up ahead.

Finally, Brunner emerges from the cornfield. He sees the children's abandoned bicycle and he notices the path.

> **MR. BRUNNER**
> This way. They went this way.

Brunner notices the large mallets lying by the work cart that is still parked in the path. He picks one up. The other men do the same.

EXT. FIELDS - NIGHT

Jennifer and Nicholas are pulling Number 4 along the path that is now running between the large fields of planted crops.

A cloud drifts before the moon and the night becomes dark.

Number 4 collapses to his knees. The waning light of his brain dims even more.

> **JENNIFER**
> — Number 4!

> **NUMBER 4**
> (Very weak)
> Jennifer... I cannot make it... back
> to the house...

Nicholas is about to cry.

> **NICHOLAS**
> Jennifer, what are we
> going to do? We can't let
> them take him apart. We
> can't.

Jennifer thinks.

> **JENNIFER**
> I know.
> (A beat)
> Okay, Nicholas, I want
> you to run down to the
> house and get Dad. Me and
> Number 4 are going to go
> hide in the fields.

> **NICHOLAS**
> But —

> **JENNIFER**
> — Do it! — Go! Or Number
> 4 will be dead before
> mornin'.

Nicholas runs off, crying. Jennifer
pulls Number 4 to his feet.

JENNIFER
Come-on Number 4. If you
wanna live you got to
try. You got to try.

They disappear into the field running
along the right hand side of the path.

EXT. FIELDS - NIGHT

Nicholas is running for all he's worth.
He trips and falls. He gets up, shaken.
He is surrounded by darkness.

NICHOLAS
Mommy...

Nicholas starts running again. He runs,
and runs, and runs. Eventually, he
disappears from sight.

EXT. FIELDS - NIGHT

Brunner and the men pass the area where
Jennifer and Number 4 had left the path.
They stop.

BLONDE MAN
I think we lost them...

Can't see them. Damn it's
dark.

Brunner looks about, searching. He
spies, deep in the field alongside them,
the dim light emanating from Number 4's
brain.

> #### MR. BRUNNER
> — There it is, in the
> field!

They run into the field.

EXT. FIELDS - NIGHT

Jennifer pulls Number 4 out of the field
they had been moving through and enters
the cornfield behind their barn.

EXT. CORNFIELD - NIGHT

Number 4 collapses to his knees.

> #### JENNIFER
> No, come-on Number 4, you
> got to get up. Look, I
> can see the barns, we're
> almost home. I can hide
> you in the cow barn.

Number 4's voice comes out slowly, his
battery near dead.

NUMBER 4
... Jenn... i... fer... please help...
me... I do... not... want to... die...

Jennifer hears Brunner and the men
approaching in the distance. She is near
tears. She manages to pull Number 4 to
his feet. Together, they stumble deeper
into the cornfield.

EXT. FIELDS - NIGHT

Brunner leads the men out of the field
and into the cornfield, following the
dim light of Number 4's brain.

EXT. CORNFIELD - NIGHT

Jennifer and Number 4 collide into the
post supporting the scarecrow. Number 4
collapses.

The clouds above move past the moon and
the night brightens. The scarecrow's
shadow appears and covers Jennifer and
Number 4.

Jennifer can hear the approaching men.
They are growing closer. She tries to
pull Number 4 to his feet but she
cannot. She begins to cry.

JENNIFER
Number 4... Number 4... I
- I'm tryin' to help you.
I'm tryin'.

NUMBER 4
I know...
        (A beat)
Jennifer...

The sound of the approaching men grows
louder. They are almost upon them.
Jennifer stops trying to pull Number 4
upright and kneels at his side, wrapping
her arms around him.

NUMBER 4
Jennifer...

JENNIFER
What?

NUMBER 4
I just... want to tell you... that...
you... are a great girl... You... will
always be... my treasure.

She hugs him tightly.

JENNIFER
Oh, Number 4.

Brunner emerges from the dark cornstalks, stepping out into the moonlight. Jennifer turns to see the other men appear at his sides. Raising their mallets, they slowly step forward.

> **MR. BRUNNER**
> Step aside girl.

> **JENNIFER**
> No, please don't hurt him... Please, he's my very best friend.

The skinny man pulls Jennifer away from Number 4. She fights him but he is much too strong for her.

> **NUMBER 4**
> ... Jennifer...

> **JENNIFER**
> No, no... Please no...

Brunner steps up to Number 4 who looks up at him with his large, round eyes that reflect the image of the man raising his hammer high above his head.

> **NUMBER 4**
> ... Goodbye Jennifer...

EXT. BANYARD - NIGHT

Nicholas runs across the barnyard, yelling.

> **NICHOLAS**
> Mommy! Daddy! Mommy!

Cleopatra starts barking.

EXT. FARMHOUSE ROOF - NIGHT

The weather vane turns slowly and then groans to a stop.

EXT. FARMHOUSE - NIGHT

Nicholas runs toward the house.

> **NICHOLAS**
> Mommy! Daddy! Mommy!

Lights in the house go on followed by Andrew, Lisa, and Clark running out into the barnyard.

> **LISA**
> Nicholas — What are you doing outside? What's wrong?

NICHOLAS
Mommy — Daddy... In the
fields, bad men. They're
trying to kill Number 4.
Jennifer's tryin' to hide
him. She told me to come
an' get you. We rescued
him from the jail!

After a stunned moment:

ANDREW
Come-on Nicholas, show me
where.

EXT. CORNFIELD - NIGHT

Jennifer is sobbing. One of Number 4's
large glass eyes is lying in front of
her.

Mr. Brunner, fatigued, drops his mallet.

Number 4's body is scattered about,
dismembered. His brain case has been
completely shattered. His brain is dark,
its pieces scattered about.

SKINNY MAN
Come-on, the things
smashed into the ground.

They hear the approach of the Reeves family, lead by their barking German Shepherd, Cleopatra.

> **BLONDE MAN**
> Yeah, let's get out of
> here.

The men leave. Brunner hesitates and then follows them, disappearing into the darkness.

Several moments pass before Cleopatra and the Reeves family emerge from the corn stalks to find Jennifer and what's left of Number 4.

Nicholas bursts into tears. Lisa gathers the children, comforting them.

Andrew sees the dark figures of the men in the distance, walking off. Clark sees them as well.

> **CLARK**
> They killed him...

> **ANDREW**
> Right in front of
> Jennifer.

Clark yells out:

CLARK
Murderers! You murderers!

Andrew puts an arm around Clark, quieting him.

ANDREW
No, no, let it go. Let it go.

EXT. FIELDS - NIGHT

Brunner continues walking off without looking back.

EXT. CORNFIELD - NIGHT

Lisa continues to comfort the children.

JENNIFER
Mom, you promised that if Number 4 ever broke or anything that Dad would fix him... as good as new.

NICHOLAS
Yeah, as good as new.

LISA
Andrew?

Andrew looks at what remains of Number 4. He shakes his head.

> **LISA**
> I'm sorry Jennifer,
> Nicholas. I'm so sorry.

> **CLARK** (O.S.)
> Wait a minute.

They turn to Clark. Clark picks up a piece of the robot's brain. It is Number 4's memory box and the micro-cortex. The pieces are still attached to one another and appear undamaged.

> **ANDREW**
> Is it damaged?

> **CLARK**
> I don't think so.

> **ANDREW**
> Then, there might be a chance.

> **LISA**
> A chance for what?

> **ANDREW**
> To bring Number 4 back to life.

NICHOLAS
But, Number 4 is dead.

Andrew takes the memory box and micro-cortex from Clark, showing it to the children.

ANDREW
Maybe not. You see, this is his memory and his thinking mind. It's what made him special. I guess you can say that this unit contains his invisible spirit. What made him alive. What made him full.

Andrew points to Number 4's scattered, dismembered parts.

ANDREW (CONTINUED)
That's not Number 4.

Andrew points to the memory box and micro-cortex.

ANDREW
This is. If we can put this into one of the other robots, as long as it's undamaged, it just might work.

> (A beat)
> But, first we have to
> call the police.

EXT. FIELD - DAWN

An empty, streamlined police car is
parked upon the dirt path that runs
between the Reeves' back fields.

EXT. CORNFIELD - DAWN

Andrew is standing beneath the field's
scarecrow with the town's balding police
officer, who is examining Number 4's
remains. He picks up one of the robot's
large glass eyes and turns it about in
his hand.

> **BALDING OFFICER**
> Well, maybe it's all for
> the best. That things
> ended this way. Now it's
> over. Brunner had his
> revenge and the people in
> town will probably feel
> better about it that way.
> I'll call the government.
> Let them know not to come
> out.

He slaps Number 4's glass eyes into
Andrew's hand.

BALDING OFFICER
You can press charges
against Brunner you know.
Trespassing, destruction
of property.

ANDREW
I won't be doing that.

BALDING OFFICER
That's good.
     (A beat)
Well, I'm going to be
heading back into town.
Goodbye Mr. Reeves.

ANDREW
Goodbye.

The officer walks off. Andrew stands
motionless for a moment and then moves
toward the barnyard at a faster than
normal pace.

INT. SMALL BARN - DAWN

Clark is installing Number 4's memory
box and micro-cortex into robot Number
5, which is seated upon a chair. Lisa
and the children are watching. Andrew
enters, joining them.

> **CLARK**
> Okay, it's connected,
> just like I did it
> before.

Andrew prepares to press the on/off
button on Number 5's torso.

> **ANDREW**
> Cross your fingers.

Andrew pushed the button. There is a
click and the robot's brain lights up.
It looks at the Reeves family.

> **NUMBER 5**
> Good morning. Today is Tuesday,
> July the sixteenth, the one
> hundred and ninety seventh day
> of this year.

The voice is completely without emotion.
Everyone is disappointed.

> **NUMBER 5** (CONTINUED)
> There are one hundred and sixty
> eight days re —

A bright spark flashes in the robot's
brain. Suddenly, he appears aware,
alive, and familiar.

NUMBER 4
Jennifer? How did I get here? How
did you save me?

Jennifer screams out in joy and leaps
forward, knocking Number 4 off his chair
and onto the floor. Squeezing him
tightly, she hugs him as hard as she
can.

JENNIFER
Oh, Number 4, I love you!
Don't you ever leave us
again. Not ever! Never!

EXT. FARMHOUSE - DAWN

Rising, the sun's morning rays warm the
farmhouse, lighting the metal weather
vane resting upon its roof. A silent
breeze blows and it turns to face the
rising star.

ENDING CREDITS

FADE OUT

Niko Zinovii

A Note from the Author

The story idea for the screenplay *Empty Eyes* materialized in this author's thoughts early one morning in 1991, while I was preparing to leave for work, at that time having been employed as a vocational rehabilitation counselor in Connecticut.

During the drive from Hartford to Meriden, I experienced in my imagination the entire movie magically unfolding in my mind. Arriving at work, I quickly wrote everything down in a detailed outline. The script was written afterward on weekends and evenings, mostly at the Wethersfield Public Library, in Connecticut. Writing *Empty Eyes* was a fulfilling experience.

The screenplay was later described and pitched to agents, production companies, and studios in Los Angeles as: The story takes place on a farm in Kansas in the near future. It's about the relationship that builds between a young girl and a robot who gains conscious awareness and the happiness, difficulties, and tragedy that results. In feel, it is reminiscent of *To Kill A Mockingbird* crossed with *Charlotte's Web*.

The script was not sold, and so no film was ever produced.

Niko Zinovii
Santa Monica, California
1 April 2020

niko@zinoviiartstudio.com

www.zinoviiartstudio.com